The Age of

The Story of a
Ms. Senior Pageant

MARY JANE BAETZ

Preface

This is a work of fiction.

It began when I entered a pageant for senior women, something that seemed like it would be fun and exciting to do. It ended as a rich experience shared with a lot of amazing women. I didn't win. I didn't receive a trophy of any kind. But I had a great time, and I got the idea for this story from that experience.

The women in this story are not real. Let me emphasize that: I made up all of the women who are in this story. Even Kate, who some might think is me, is not real, she is not me. As far as I know there is no Ms. Senior Tri-Rivers Pageant, and there is no Tri-Rivers region. I made them up. However, the experience I had competing for the title of Queen was real and is at the heart of this story.

The only other thing that is real is the fabulous black Mardi Gras gown, the one on the cover of this book. I really did buy it on line. It really is a vintage dress. And I really did love wearing it in the pageant.

~ Mary Jane Baetz

Table of Contents

IN THE BEGINNING
Start With Your Face 2
The Invitation 5
The Decision 10
On Your Mark, Get Set 16
A Gown Fit for a Queen 26

Week 1
SATURDAY, MARCH 8
Kick-Off Meeting 32
Goodbyes and Hellos 49

Week 2
SATURDAY, MARCH 15
The First Rehearsal 56
Philosophies and Other Words 73
Hair, the Crowning Glory 91

Week 3
SATURDAY, MARCH 22
Costumes and Talent 98
An Online Experience 142

Week 4
SATURDAY, MARCH 29
Myrna and the Merry Widow 148
Getting the Gowns On 153
Modeling the Gowns 164

Gown Photos 171
Everyone Has a Story 174
Getting to Know You Luncheon..................... 181
A Matter of Time 207

Week 5
SATURDAY, APRIL 5
Realities................................ 212
Black and White Discovery 218
Step by Step to the Finale 228

Week 6
FRIDAY, APRIL 11 and SATURDAY, APRIL 12
Interviews With the Judges........................... 236
Pageant Day - Saturday, April 12.................... 243
Let the Show Begin 255
A Whole Lot of Talent, and More.................. 264
Regrets, Apologies, and Curtain Calls............ 275
And the Winner Is 278
Good Night Ladies 293

AFTER THE PAGEANT
Post-Pageant Party.......................... 298
Was It Worth It? 305

About Ms. Senior Pageants 308

In the Beginning

Start With Your Face

Kevin bent down to study Kate Dearborn's face as she sat in a swivel chair, a lavender bib draped across her chest and fastened behind her neck. He didn't look pleased.

"She's really pale," he pronounced to Shirley Mortenson, who had accompanied Kate to Kevin's Salon in Devonville to purchase makeup and learn how to wear it. "She needs color, a good foundation." With a general wave of his hand he said, "She can't go on stage looking like that!"

Kate blinked. After all, she was sitting right there in front of him but he spoke to Shirley, not to her. He stood up, placing his hand on his hip. "You know she'll never be Queen unless we fix her!" Kate could hardly contain her smile. They looked her over like she was an empty page and agreed if she were to be crowned Queen in just a few weeks her face would require a whole lot of makeup, skillfully and artfully applied.

Kevin leaned down again, taking a closer look at Kate's forehead. Still speaking to Shirley he said, "Look at her eyebrows. She's got nothing!" He shook his head in despair. "She's not going to like this. She has to have some eyebrows." He reached up and opened a cupboard, pulled down a huge box marked 'samples' and put it on the table beside Kate.

While Kevin dug through the box, Shirley moved closer and examined Kate's forehead. "What happened to your eyebrows?" she asked.

"Nothing happened," Kate answered. "They just sort of fell out as I got older. My Mom's eyebrows did the same thing."

Suspicious, Shirley whispered, "You didn't pluck them out?"

Kate whispered back, "No, I didn't pluck them. They fell out. My eyebrows went bald. Sometimes things go bald when you get old."

Waving a fat little pencil in his hand, Kevin studied Kate's face. In a moment he began sketching. The Midnight Taupe Wonder Pencil flew furiously back and forth across her brow as he lectured, "You can't have bald eyebrows. The 'in' look today in all the magazines is big bushy eyebrows. This will fix them." More furious drawing, creating one eyebrow then the other. "There," he said triumphantly.

He stepped back so Kate could look in the mirror. Startled, the only thing she could mutter was, "Oh. Look at those eyebrows."

Next he squeezed a blob of Barely Nude Ivory Perfection Foundation onto his fingertips, dabbed it on Kate's chin, and stroked it up and over her face.

"Yes, yes, yes, this is better," he said approvingly.

Searching through the box of samples again, Kevin selected a tiny jar of Smokey Mountain Eye Shadow and a compact of Fresh Baked Peach Blush which he placed on the table along with several fluffy brushes. He studied her face again. "These will do wonders," he predicted.

Kevin and Shirley were hard at work getting Kate's face ready to compete in the Ms. Senior Tri-Rivers Pageant.

Kate was having a ball.

The Invitation

It happened at a ladies writing club one March morning where the discussion was the usual "how to develop new characters and new ideas." The group met from 9 to 11 a.m. on the first Tuesday of every month. Over the years together some of the ladies had written articles for newsletters and journals, and some had published a short story or two. One member had self-published a guide called *Discovering Your Ancestry*; another had published a memoire about her two years in the Peace Corps during the 1970s. That morning the discussion turned to how a good description improves a narrative. The members shared how some people surprise us with where they've lived, the things they've done, and elements of their lives we never knew about. The question was how do we find out these things, these unique phases of people's lives?

Shirley Mortenson attended the meeting, a first-time guest. She suggested it. The Pageant. Looking around at the group, she asked if there was anyone who would consider entering a competition for senior women, a Ms. Senior Tri-Rivers competition. "That," she declared, "would be a story! There," she continued, "you will find fascinating women whose stories will enrich and deepen your writing. They," she proclaimed, "are women whose lives you might never know about and suddenly during the pageant, their talents and interests and philosophies of life are on parade."

She wasn't quite finished. "And you," she concluded, "will surprise yourself. You will dig deep as a competitor in ways you cannot even imagine. How about it? Who among you is daring enough, curious enough or just plain crazy enough to enter the Ms. Senior Tri-Rivers Pageant?"

Silence filled the room. No one moved for fear it would look as if she was the one willing to take the challenge. "Come on," encouraged Shirley. She turned to Kate and held out a business card. "How about you? Will you consider being a candidate for Ms. Senior Tri-Rivers?" she asked, slipping the card into Kate's hand.

"Me? What?" replied a very bemused Kate. "I've never heard of it. I have no idea what it would require. Not me!" Flustered, Kate recalled that when everyone in the room routinely introduced themselves, this lady identified herself first as Shirley Mortenson, but then as Ms. Senior Tri-Rivers, a title she'd held seven years ago. She stated her name and title, then smiled and added "and I'm 71." Being the next person at the table, Kate smiled and gave her

own name and age: "I'm Kate Dearborn, and I'm 73."
She surprised herself. That was something new for
Kate. She normally refrained from such open disclo-
sure about her age, but Shirley made it seem so easy,
it just sort of happened.

That might explain why Shirley had her eye on
Kate. It probably had a lot to do with what Kate said.
"I was just playing," she tried to explain. "When you
said your age, I said mine!"

It was too late. By now the other writing club
members sided with Shirley. "Yes, Kate, you would
be great."

And even though she said No, No, No, Kate
wasn't very convincing because Shirley continued,
saying, "Really, Kate, I hope you will consider it. We
are looking for candidates who are elegant women,
age 60 and up. The competition for a new Ms. Senior
Tri-Rivers is in April. It's just six weeks away. We are
looking for women who exemplify what we call The
Age of Elegance. You are perfect."

The rest of the women gleefully agreed. "Yes!
We will all come to the pageant and cheer you on!"
Oh my, the praise they heaped upon Kate, urging her
to compete for Ms. Senior Tri-Rivers. While some
of the praise probably originated in the relief they
felt not to be the chosen one, they also believed Kate
would be a fine candidate. With great enthusiasm
they encouraged her.

"You'll get to wear a gown, something really beautiful!"

"And a crown, a Queen's crown!"

"You will perform a talent, you know that, don't you? Can you sing?"

"And makeup. Can you put on eye shadow and blush and all of that? My cousin is a beautician, maybe she could help."

"What about your hair, you must do something with your hair! Can you twist it into a bun or something?"

Everyone implored Kate to compete, all the while enjoying the diversion from normal writing club discussions.

Before they left the meeting, Shirley urged her once more. "Check it out at *www.msseniortririvers.com*, no spaces, no dashes. It's a wonderful experience. At least think about it, will you?"

Kate tucked the card into her purse and promised, "Yes, I will."

It was nearly 11:30 a.m. when the meeting came to an end. The members picked up their notebooks, put on their jackets and said their goodbyes. Driving home, Kate supposed thoughts of the age of elegance were probably quickly forgotten by the others as they went on their way to the grocery store, to babysit a grandchild, or other activities, but was surprised to find that her own thoughts about the Ms. Senior

Tri-Rivers Pageant were still with her. As she drove down the hill a funny thing happened. The song "Age of Aquarius" began going through her head, but she substituted, "age of elegance," and even though she noticed, as a writer, that the syllables didn't quite fit the tune, she thought it was a great way to say age sixty and up. Or 73.

The code name for "old" was very nice: The Age of Elegance.

The Decision

At home, Kate greeted her little dog, Lolita. "Hey," she said, picking her up and rubbing her head. "Let's go see how elegant I am, shall we?"

She walked into the bedroom to take a long look in the mirror. "Not exactly a beauty but not too bad," she said as Lolita wagged. Turning around to examine her other side, she nodded, "I look elegant enough."

It had been only an hour since she left the writing club meeting, and now she was seriously pondering the idea of entering a pageant. She tried explaining to herself there was no reason she needed to do this, as in the old days when it would look good on her resume. She told herself that winning this will not get her a scholarship or a grant. She graduated from college, and got a good job without ever winning a title. Not one. She worked hard, moved up and eventually rose to the position of Director of Communications without ever being Ms. Senior Tri-Rivers. Remember, she said to herself, you won't win a cruise, not even a weekend vacation. In fact, you have to pay money to do this. And you have to donate your time, your precious time. On the other hand, perhaps as a writer you will find a good story or two, something for a hometown newspaper, although she seriously wondered if anyone would really care about a bunch of old ladies competing for a title.

She took the card out of her purse and studied the words, The Age of Elegance. Okay, she said to herself, let's be honest. After everything you just said to yourself, why would you do this? The answers came easily. There is something tantalizing and glamorous about entering a pageant, especially for a 73-year-old woman who is retired and can do pretty much whatever she wants. And truthfully, her life these days was pretty quiet and uneventful. That's not all bad, being quiet and uneventful, she reminded herself. She smiled at her knack for talking to herself, although not out loud. Yet. She continued, Dear God, there is not a day that I am not fully aware and grateful for the good life I am so privileged to live. But, and here came the kicker, but doing this, entering a pageant with a bunch of old ladies – she decided to reword that – I mean ladies of the age of elegance – doing this could be the most exciting thing I've done for a long time!

Breathing a big sigh of relief for having worked through her thoughts, she amused herself with visions of a beautiful gown and makeup. She ignored the hair issue, as she had no idea what to do with that. She tried to remember the last time she thought about wearing a gown and high heels. It had been years. Maybe she thought about high heels and pretty gowns back in the days when she and Jim were married. Maybe, but probably not. They were so young, just barely out of college and didn't have the money to dress up and go out and about, she recalled, but that was another story. Normally she would not even think about being married, it was so long ago. And yet, on occasions like this she would imagine Jim in Los Angeles and the glamorous lifestyle he lived.

She tried not to think of him often because when she did, she still felt a twinge of sadness remembering those days of their youth, days when Jim couldn't find a job related to his degree in theatre arts. He tried. For a while he took some small jobs just to make ends meet, but it was acting and directing he wanted to do, and that was not available to him in this small town. He wanted to follow his dream. He wanted Kate to go with him, but back then it all seemed so uncertain, and of course she had just started a good job, so she couldn't imagine leaving everything for Hollywood, of all things! Hollywood seemed foolish and impossible.

In time it was Jim who made the decision. Again he asked Kate to go with him. He begged her. They both cried. But she took the safe route:

she stayed. She was sure he would find out that Hollywood was not what he thought. She would wait for him. She believed he would come back. He never did, and after a year they divorced. He was gone forever.

Sometimes she would hear about him, usually a scrap of news from someone they both knew. He married a young actress, and things were good for them for a while. Then they divorced. He married again, divorced, and then married again. His total was four marriages, including his with Kate. Along the way he stopped being Jim and became James. He made a good career for himself, mostly as a director, not an actor.

Kate never married again and eventually returned to her maiden name, Kate Dearborn. Her life was satisfying, her health was good, and she was financially secure. Then today at a writing club, of all things, suddenly there was this opportunity for a fling, an adventure, an opportunity to dress up and get out there again. She pushed the melancholy and fleeting thoughts of Jim out of her mind, as she always did. Now she needed to concentrate on this alluring adventure in her otherwise comfortable life.

Her head swirled with ideas. She summarized one more time, just to be sure. There would be a gown competition. Interviews with judges. A talent show. Gulp. There it was again: talent. That could be a problem, she thought. She was not sure she had any talent since abandoning piano lessons in the second grade and giving up dancing after a stint as a junior high school cheerleader. How would her career in communications yield a talent for the stage? She needed to think some more about the talent aspect. Imagine me, an old Queen, she thought. Ooops, do I need to be careful about that? Do I need to be politically correct? Should I say former Queen? Get over it, Kate admonished herself, we are not talking PC things here. And at 73 the idea of being an old Queen and having such fun sounds ridiculous, far-fetched and just great.

After changing into sweatpants and a flannel shirt, she sat down at the computer and googled Ms. Senior Tri-Rivers. Scrolling through pages of photos of glamorous, smiling ladies adorned with sashes and sparkling tiaras, she finally found the current information. There it was: six weeks of preparation and practice prior to the Ms. Senior Tri-Rivers Pageant. The final evening would feature elegant ladies in beautiful gowns, talent performances from all of the contestants, a local radio announcer as MC, and guest performances by former Queens. The winner – the new Queen – would be crowned at that gala event. She would assume the title of Ms. Senior Tri-Rivers and would represent senior women of The Age of Elegance in the Tri-Rivers region for the next year.

At the bottom of the page it said, "Call Harriet Anderson, Pageant Chair, for complete details and an entry application." Kate Dearborn picked up the phone and called her.

On Your Mark, Get Set...

Harriet Anderson offered to send out the information right away. "I'll get it to the Post Office by 5:30 p.m. for the last pickup today," she promised, explaining that the kick-off meeting was scheduled for the coming weekend and she was sure Kate would want to be there.

True to her word, the next day, Wednesday, a large envelope inscribed with a Ms. Senior Tri-Rivers logo arrived in Kate's mailbox. She tore it open and pulled out a letter, several forms and instruction sheets, a couple of pamphlets, and a souvenir sticker in the shape of a crown with her name neatly hand printed on it: KATE. She stuck it on the inside cover of her calendar book. She still carried a regular paper calendar, even though everyone else seemed to use smart phones or iPads to keep their dates in order. At age 73 it was hard to give up the old-fashioned way of writing down dates in a calendar. Kate liked the look of that crown when she opened the book and besides, you can't put a sticker in your phone, she reasoned.

She emptied the contents of the envelope onto the dining room table, wondering what she was about to get herself into. There were two things in particular she wanted to know about: the cost of being a candidate and the schedule of activities. She would make note of each area as she proceeded.

- **Application and Entry Fee**
  - Complete the application form, including all biographical information.
  - $99 non-refundable entry fee.
  - Submit both in advance or turn them in at the kick-off meeting.

- **Formal Studio Portrait (not a snapshot)**
  - A portrait taken by a professional photographer. This will be used for publicity, the webpage, and the pageant program. Make your appointment soon. The names of two suggested portrait photographers are included.

- **Gown, Costume, and Special Clothes**
  - Formal gown, coordinating shoes, jewelry and accessories.
  - Attire for the interview with the judges, coordinating shoes and accessories.
  - Costume to wear for your talent competition, including shoes and accessories.
  - Black and white combo to wear for the opening of the pageant. *(See separate page for complete details and guidelines.)*

- Cosmetics and hair products, including all makeup items necessary to wear with all of the above outfits.

Kate paused to find the separate page with the guidelines for the black and white clothes. Reviewing it quickly, she noted that she already had several items in her closet to choose from: white blouse or knit top, black skirt or slacks, black shoes. There was no need to start a search now for the black and white costume. Relieved, she put a paper clip on the page to remind her to review it as the competition got closer.

General Information, Dates and Times

- Contestants must be present for every rehearsal, the whole time. You may be excused for health reasons or family emergencies, but that must be explained to Harriet Anderson, and she will excuse you. Once you are accepted into the pageant, you must attend weekly rehearsals. Sign here.
- **Saturday March 8, 10 a.m.**
  - Kick-off meeting. Bring your questions, meet other contestants, and turn in your application to be sure you are signed up.
- **Saturday, March 15, 8 a.m. – 12 noon**
  - Philosophy of Life practice

- Shoe practice, walking on stage - high heeled shoes required

- **Saturday, March 22, 8 a.m. – 12 noon**
  - Talent practice
  - Talent costume required for practice and approval

- **Saturday, March 29, 8 a.m. – 1:30 p.m.**
  - Modeling practice - Pageant gowns required for practice and approval
  - Philosophy of Life practice
  - Luncheon – "Getting to Know You"

- **Saturday, April 5, 8 a.m. – noon**
  - Opening/closing practice - Black and white costumes required for practice and approval
  - Review of Crowning Ceremony

- **Friday, April 11, 5 - 9 p.m.**
  (the evening before the pageant)
  - Interviews with the judges
    Location: Neighborhood Inn
    Every contestant must be present for the entire time, even though each interview will be limited to only five minutes.

- **Saturday, April 12, 10 a.m. - 9:30 p.m.**
  PAGEANT DAY
  Three Rivers Performing Arts Center
  - Full day of practice:

> Philosophy of Life
> Gowns
> Talent
> Opening/Closing
> Crowning

- Lunch

- Makeup and Hair

- Photos

- Media interviews

- Pageant begins at 6 p.m.
  The pageant is a 2½ hour event where
  the new Queen is crowned. (Plan for the
  program to end at about 9 p.m. just in case
  it runs long.)

- Celebration Party 9 – 10 p.m.
  Stay for the celebration backstage at the
  Performing Arts Center. Family and friends
  welcome!

- Motel Accommodations
  For those contestants who wish to make
  reservations for a night or two in a nearby
  motel, we have arranged for special rates.
  Names of motels included. Mention the
  pageant for special rates.

Kate paused to reflect. Three Rivers
Performing Arts Center is located in the geographical

center of the widespread cities and communities of the region. It's a beautiful location, but a location almost 70 miles from her home in the community of Northridge. To be at the Center at eight in the morning meant she would need to be on the road by 6:30 a.m. and hope for no traffic problems. When the rehearsal ended at mid-day, Kate would drive the 70 miles home through the Saturday traffic with people out shopping, taking their kids to soccer games, or heading out of town. All of this spelled a commitment to give a great deal of one precious commodity: Time.

As the years passed she found herself more aware of the passing of time and was more inclined to evaluate how she spent her time. Kate asked herself if she really wanted to spend her time this way. Was she willing to give up beautiful mornings at home to battle her way down the highway? Was she willing to spend hours in a rehearsal hall or restaurant when she could be out walking with her dog or snuggled at home on her sofa, enjoying a book or a movie? When you are young, time seems endless and stretches beyond where you can possibly imagine; you are certain there will be plenty of time to do whatever you want. But at some age, whether it is 50 or 60 or 70, time becomes as precious as money, probably more precious. Kate, like so many others, considered carefully how she was willing to spend it.

She opened her calendar book, glancing at the KATE sticker as she turned to the month of March.

Using a pencil (so it could be erased, she reasoned), she began with March 8 and crossed through each of the days required for the Ms. Senior Tri-Rivers rehearsals, knowing that the time for travel plus the time needed to relax and recuperate would easily account for long, full days. Next she crossed out the Friday evening interview date. Finally she put a big X through the entire Saturday of the pageant itself, April 12, and Sunday, the day after, just so she could plan on a day of rest. Suddenly those weeks were becoming very full.

Now she crossed out a couple of other days each week to remind herself that there was shopping to be done and most important, time to devote to developing, practicing and perfecting her talent, whatever that was going to be, and her philosophy of life to be delivered in just thirty seconds. Was that possible, she wondered. A whole life philosophy in thirty seconds? It would take time to work that out. It was clear that the commitment was not just for a one-shot pageant, it was for a minimum of two or three days a week for the next six weeks. It was conceivable it could add up to even more. And she thought she was retired! She laughed at herself.

Had Kate known what else was required of a Tri-Rivers Queen, she might have laughed harder, or perhaps she would have simply erased the pencil marks, closed the calendar and walked away. What she didn't know yet was that being Queen meant there would be dozens of additional crossed out days and many more miles of travel in numbers she could not begin to quantify. She did not fully realize how much time the new Queen, the new Ms. Senior Tri-Rivers, would be required to give in the year ahead. As Harriet Anderson would tell everyone early on, "When you are the Queen, we own you." She would pause to let it sink in.

"I repeat. We own you. Really."

What she meant became perfectly clear. "You will be on call every single day for a year. There will be meetings, openings, expos, community fairs, parades, interviews, and lots of performances, especially at events for seniors. You will travel all over the Tri-Rivers region, in your own car, driving yourself. You will be the spokesperson and representative of elegant women throughout the Tri-Rivers. We may call you on a Monday and tell you to be at an opening on Tuesday. We may call you in the morning and expect you to be somewhere in an hour, so get used to carrying your cell phone, your crown, and your gown in your car. Keep your hair and makeup in ready-to-go condition. Carry a suitcase in your car stocked with costumes and extra makeup for last minute requests. If you are the Queen, there will be no vacation for you during the year. Last year's Queen made 103 appearances. And at the end of your reign, you will participate in a national competition for the title of Ms. Senior America, almost a week of travel and competition. Be prepared for this commitment. It's for real, and it's a lot of time."

Kate and the other candidates would hear this and ponder it. Some would see it as an opportunity to fill their days with happy moments. Others would see it as daunting and decide to drop out of such a demanding schedule. When you are 60-plus, and time has become a very precious commodity, you must consider carefully where and how you spend it.

Kate's phone rang. It was her sister Colleen in Chicago. "Hi Kate, what's happening?" There was always a smile in her voice which made Kate smile too.

Kate told her about the pageant, beginning with the woman at the writing club who handed her a business card. "It seemed sort of crazy but then I started thinking about it, and now I am actually seriously considering it," Kate told her sister.

"That's awesome! Do it Kate, do it! I will come down to cheer for you. Maybe Megan can come too. Do it!" Colleen always cheered her on and felt great pride for everything Kate did. She was a big fan. Megan was her daughter.

"Well, it will take a lot of time, so I am still not fully committed. And it will cost a lot of money. There are so many things I will need to buy, like a gown, makeup, shoes, and that's just the beginning."

"Come on," Colleen urged her in her in a serious voice. "You can afford it. Stop worrying about the money for heaven's sake. As for the time, we all deal with that at our age. Think of it as an opportunity to use your time for something special. Really Kate, how many opportunities do you have to do something like this?" With a big smile in her voice, she added, "This will be fun for you, and knowing you, you'll probably win."

"It would be fun to win," Kate said, "but I don't know..." She had not begun the quest to become Queen quite yet. First she needed to decide if she was going to enter the pageant.

She promised Colleen she would think it through and make a decision very soon.

She hung up the phone and stacked the papers beside the envelope. It seemed like a good time for a little break. "Here, Lolita," she called to her ever patient dog. "Let's go for a walk!" As if Lolita understood every word, she added, "We will worry about this tomorrow." Lolita wagged. Kate smiled, thinking this might be how Scarlett felt in *Gone With the Wind*.

A Gown Fit for a Queen

Kate made the decision the next morning, Thursday, and sent an email to Colleen to let her know. "It's an adventure," she wrote. "Something about the serious yet not-so-serious pursuit of a crown has always appealed to women, and I guess I am no different. Thanks for your encouragement!"

Kate knew that in the past she would not have ventured into such unknown territory. In the past she preferred to know the path she would take. But this event felt safe. She wondered if it was because she was older and more comfortable. Or perhaps it was because she would be with women her own age. Whatever the reason, it was tantalizing to imagine being glamorous, it was challenging to see how well she would do in a competition, and it was exciting to push herself to try something so different. Maybe somewhere in the whole experience she would find a good story to write, she told herself, and of course all of it sounded like fun!

"Now," she explained to Lolita who sat nearby, hoping for a walk, "now I need to get to work. We will take a walk in a few minutes. Be patient." She found the business card from Shirley Mortenson, picked up the phone, and called her.

"Yes! That's what I was hoping you would say!" Shirley exclaimed. "Sometime soon, let's go to my favorite salon to see Kevin. He does all of my makeup and my hair. He would love to help you. I mean help you to be Queen. You will love him!" Kate thanked her and said she would call her soon to make some arrangements.

Next she filled out all the forms, wrote a check, and made an appointment for a portrait. She decided her talent would be a poetry recitation. She would select a beautiful, meaningful poem by some wonderful American poet, memorize it, and present it to the audience. Who would it be, she asked herself. Emily Dickinson? Robert Frost? Sylvia Plath? No, not Plath, she decided quickly, too dark, too disturbing. Walt Whitman? Edgar Allan Poe? No, not Poe either, she reasoned with herself. Too dark, too. She would get back to that. She jotted down some ideas for the section of the competition called Philosophy of Life. Her quest to be Queen had begun, and to her, the most exciting part was just ahead: finding a gown.

Kate knew she must begin the search immediately. It was already Thursday and the first meeting was on Saturday, March 8. She tried to imagine what her gown would be like, but that was difficult. All she could be sure of was that it would be glamorous, long, sparkling, and beautiful. After all, weren't all pageant gowns beautiful? Holding that thought, she put on her jacket and took Lolita for a nice walk, as promised. After they came back she grabbed her purse and keys and hurried to the car. Time to go shopping! Little did she know it would be the first of many excursions she would make in search of a gown.

As Kate entered The Bon Marche downtown, she tried to remember the last time she was here. It had been a while. She took the escalator to the second floor where a clerk greeted her and asked how she could help.

"I am looking for a gown, a pageant gown, something long and glamorous," she said, hoping this would be sufficient information.

"A pageant gown?" squealed the clerk, her eyes flashing. "How exciting!" Sweeping her arm toward the racks of inventory, she half-asked, half-exclaimed, "For your granddaughter? We have tons of gowns she would love: strapless, halter, hi-lo, slinky, skinny," she pronounced with a broad smile.

"No," Kate smiled sweetly back at her, "it's for me."

For just a split second the clerk's smile turned to surprise, or maybe it was alarm. She must have been about 19 years old, and Kate must have seemed quite ancient to her. It must have been beyond her wildest thoughts to think that Kate would need a pageant gown for herself. "I see," blinked the clerk. Then she quickly looked around the vast floor as if to figure out what she could do for Kate. "Perhaps something from the Mother of the Bride selection?" she suggested, gesturing across to the bridal section.

"No, nothing like that," Kate said, refusing to leave the formals. "I want a pageant gown that has some real pizzazz." Kate wondered if the clerk knew what pizzazz was, or was that word old fashioned. Kate decided it was best to just repeat what would become her mantra: "A glamorous, long, sparkling, beautiful gown – for me," she said.

Still smiling sweetly, the pretty young clerk shuffled through the racks of dresses. Her description of each dress became a question as she held out one at a time. A long orange shimmering gown slit up to the hip? A strapless black satin sweetheart top with layers of golden ruffles attached to the waist? A red slinky halter top worn without a bra? For the next fifteen minutes Kate shook her head. No thanks. I don't think so. No, not that one. No, no, sorry - no. Finally Kate thanked the clerk, picked up her purse, and took the escalator down. As she left the store she made a quick mental note: not one suitable dress for her in all of The Bon Marche. It could be a long hunt.

Back home, Kate pulled out the packet of information so she could review the timetable for getting everything done on schedule. A gown was not required until the fourth week, March 29. However, Harriet Anderson urged everyone to start their search early. Now the reason became clear. It would take time to find a gown.

The next day was Friday, the day before the kick-off meeting. Kate stopped by the thrift store where she volunteered twice a month. She recalled that once she had seen a gown there which appeared to be nearly new. Maybe it had been worn to a prom, or perhaps to a holiday party, and then the owner gave it away. Kate wanted to ask the manager to watch for a gown like that for her.

"Let me get this straight," smiled the manager. "You think you will find some sort of pageant gown here in a thrift store? Well, that would be just short of a miracle!" The manager chuckled before she continued. "Let me be serious for a minute. What exactly is your size and what is the style you think would suit you?" Folding her arms, she waited for Kate's answer.

"It would be a medium or a large, a size 12 or so, and it would be glamorous, long, sparkling, and beautiful."

"Uh huh, okay" answered the skeptical manager, nodding. She pledged to keep an eye out for that perfect dress. Kate realized this did not sound promising so she put the idea aside. Her quest for a gown would have to wait.

Saturday,
March 8

Kick-off Meeting

Saturday morning was clear and cool, and Kate was ready to drive to the Three Rivers Performing Arts Center, some 70 miles away. First, Kate needed to take care of her dog. "Lolita, come on. We're going to the Doggie Resort." The five-year-old puppy understood and wiggled and waited for her leash. With six Saturdays of rehearsals ahead, Lolita would need some good care. She would have fun at doggie resort while Kate was off prancing around in a gown. As soon as they checked in, Lolita rushed off to play with the other dogs. "See you later," Kate waved as the wagging tail disappeared across the yard.

Kate arrived at the center and entered the auditorium a few minutes before ten o'clock. From where she sat, she was able to see most of the people as they came in. With the great acoustics in the auditorium, it wasn't hard to hear them, either. Some clustered together talking and laughing, while others sat quietly by themselves.

Across the room at a side exit, two women entered together, both of them wearing light rain jackets, talking as if they were old friends. "Stop worrying, Rosemarie, I locked the car," said the

woman with the plain brown hair and headband, reassuring the other. She held a dark green tote bag in
one hand, and a set of keys in the other.

"Okay, Stephanie. Let's sit over there, or there,"
said her plump friend with the thick white hair, who
pointed and gestured with dramatic emphasis, first
one way then the other, trying to pick out seats. Still
holding the car keys in her hand, Stephanie calmly
followed her.

A tall woman with long blond-gray hair arrived
with a balding man about her age. Laughing and
talking as they searched for seats, they finally decided
to sit at the side of the auditorium. She could be
heard proudly introducing herself and the man to a
couple of women seated nearby.

"Hi! My name is Anita. This is my husband, Mr.
Nick. He can explain how he got that name, not me.
I'm just the wife," she laughed. "We are excited about
this competition, especially Mr. Nick. This whole
thing was actually his idea. Like I said, I'm just the
wife." She winked when she said it.

The two women introduced themselves as Olga
and Jane. Both of them agreed they were also excited
about the competition. "Both of us are dancers, or
at least Olga is," said Jane as they introduced themselves. "How about you?"

Mr. Nick answered. "Anita plays a real mean
piano. We couldn't exactly bring hers along but

they tell us there is one on stage. Can't wait to see it. I mean hear it. I mean play it. You know what I mean!"

Anita shook her head and rolled her eyes. "Men."

Kate continued to look around the auditorium to see who else was there, who was arriving. The seats were plentiful, and the small audience was scattered. Way to the front, in the second row, a woman sat alone, relaxed and observant. Of medium build with rich black skin, she wore a simple hairdo pulled back in a French twist, and a lightweight ivory wool jacket with a silk scarf under the collar. Seated in the same row, just two seats away, another woman seemed to be contemplating the whole experience. Wearing a burgundy colored jacket and a matching lightweight wool beret, her face was exceptionally serene as she waited for the program to begin.

"Hello, I'm Angeline," said the black woman, smiling at her.

"Hello," the woman answered, "I'm Helen." They didn't say anything more until a slender blonde woman slipped into a seat at the end of the row.

"Hello," she said, "I'm Sherry. Sherry Springfield." She lowered her eyes and did not seem to hear the other two women say hello back to her.

In a row toward the rear of the audience, a man wearing jeans, a gray sweatshirt, and a baseball cap struck up a conversation with another man who was sitting with his wife. "Yeah, I've been a Yankee fan my whole life," he said, pointing to his NY Yankees hat.

"Hey, you can have the Yankees, I'll stick with the Rockies," said the husband, pointing to his own cap. "My wife here, Carol, she could care less." Carol paid no attention to either of the men as she looked around at the other women in the audience.

In a few minutes, the Yankee fan was joined by a petite redhead who announced loudly, "Hi, I'm Myrna. Excuse me. I was in the ladies room. We drove all the way over from Northridge this morning after two cups of coffee!"

Seated nearby was another woman who laughed heartily at Myrna's comment. "You're lucky you got coffee! I barely made it out of bed, but at least I'm here. I'm Bonnie."

A man wearing a large camera on a strap around his neck put down a big black satchel and began to set up photographic equipment in the center aisle. He turned to greet a woman walking with the assistance of a cane as she entered the row in front of him.

"Hello. May I take your coat for you?" he offered.

"Thanks, I'm Judith Ann. Looking at all of your supplies and equipment, I'd say you must be our photographer."

"Nice to meet you, Judith Ann" he replied, arranging her coat over the back of a chair. "Yes, I am Dave, your official photographer. This is my first day but you'll be seeing a lot of me in the weeks ahead. All the way to the Ms. Senior Tri-Rivers Pageant next month." Gesturing to a lady seated three seats in, he said, "This is Sandi, we just met too."

A woman wearing cowboy boots, blue jeans, and a caramel-colored leather jacket took a seat in the same row as Kate. She fidgeted with her jacket and looked around the auditorium.

Kate spoke first. "Hello, are you here for the pageant?" Kate suddenly felt a little silly. Wasn't it obvious she was here for the pageant? Weren't most of the women who came to the meeting here for the pageant? Maybe this was her first case of nerves, Kate thought to herself. "I'm Kate Dearborn, from Northridge," she said.

To Kate's great relief, the woman stretched out her hand and said, "Hi, I'm Teresa Rodriguez. Me too." Then they both sat there, silent. Raising her eyebrows and with a shrug of her shoulders Teresa added, "Sorry. 'Me too' sounds a little silly, doesn't it? I mean I am here for the pageant too. But I am not from Northridge. I guess I am a little nervous. I am just not quite sure how to get started with this," she smiled.

"Me too!" laughed Kate. "What do you say –
shall we both just relax and start again?"

"Great idea! I'll start by using a cowgirl phrase,"
she laughed, pointing to her own cowboy boots.
"How did you get roped into this, Kate?"

Kate briefly explained that she was no cowgirl
but had simply been invited by a woman at her
writing club. "How about you, Teresa? Let me ask
you the same thing: how did you get roped into this?"

Teresa shrugged, "Well, it wasn't my idea.
My kids told me about it. They saw an ad in the
newspaper. You know how kids are, they like the
idea, but I'm not so sure. They think I've been a
widow sitting at home out on our little ranch long
enough." She paused.

Kate sensed that perhaps Teresa did not want
to go on. Maybe this conversation was still off to an
awkward start. She decided the best thing to do was
to wait until it felt comfortable to continue. It was
only a couple of seconds until Teresa spoke again,
almost a whisper.

"My husband, Luis – he died two years ago."

Impulsively, Kate reached out to touch her
shoulder, not even wondering if it would be okay
with her. "I'm sorry," Kate said, and Teresa did not
seem to mind.

"No, I'm sorry," Teresa answered. "It just sort of
slipped out. I didn't really plan to say that."

"It's okay, really it is," said Kate.

Teresa's voice was a little more audible now. "It's been difficult but I'm dealing with it. Luis was my rock. He really believed in me. We have a little place we call *Rancho Rico*. You know, *rico* means rich in Spanish, and believe me, we felt rich to have such a nice little place. We lived there with our two kids and maintained it all. He had another job in town that paid the bills, so he had two jobs and worked really hard. But even when things were tough, he always believed everything would be okay. He always reminded me that we could handle almost anything, but that was when he was here. He was gone too soon. You never know how life will go. He was with us one morning and gone that night. Aortic aneurysm, it's like a heart attack."

"I am so sorry. I bet he was a great guy," Kate said, thinking how different her own life experience had been.

"He was," Teresa answered. "We used to have a little trio, he played the piano, I played guitar, and we had a drummer. We sang all sorts of songs, lots of Western music but a lot of other songs too. We did little gigs for friends at weddings and parties, things like that, playing all sorts of music. We had a great time, but I haven't sung like that since he died. Our kids, my son and daughter, they think I need to get my life started again. Like I don't have a good life with my horses and dogs? They've said to me more than once that their dad, Luis, would love to see me do this. They say he would love to hear me sing again, and he would be out here cheering me on."

Teresa was one of those women some would call ageless, although she was required to be 60-and-up to meet the criteria for Ms. Senior Tri-Rivers. Her dark hair was thick with tight springy waves. It was long enough to clip back in a ponytail, but even then springy curls pulled free around her face. Her swept back hair revealed a network of horizontal and vertical lines, probably from squinting in the sun over the years outside at the ranch. Her physique was trim and athletic. Kate quickly concluded this petite woman, dressed in her casual yet elegant way, was one of the most attractive women in the audience.

"My kids think it would be great for me to get out of my denims and into some nicer clothes. In a way, they seem to think that changing my clothes might help me change my life. They love the idea of me in a gown! Me in a gown? Well, let me put it this way, it's kind of an issue. I am not sure what they are thinking, but wearing a fancy dress just isn't my idea of fun."

She shook her head, then turned the conversation to Kate. "How about you, Kate? Have you ever worn a gown? Have you found one for the pageant?"

Kate thought about her search so far. "No, I've

never worn one either," she replied. "I'm still looking
for something I like. It's not easy, but you will
probably find something you'll like too."

Teresa frowned. "I really don't think so. Like
I said, it's kind of an issue. And besides, what I like
are boots and jeans. But I'll stay long enough today
to tell my kids I was here, then maybe they will leave
me alone."

The auditorium lights dimmed and the room got
quiet. A spotlight centered on the curtains, which
slowly parted. Wearing a lacy silver gown and a
white satin banner that read "Ms. Senior Tri-Rivers,"
a petite woman with perfectly styled silver-white
hair stepped forward, waving and smiling. "Hello
and welcome! I am Harriet Anderson and this is
the kick-off meeting for the Ms. Senior Tri-Rivers
Pageant. We are so glad you are here!"

Everyone clapped. It was the first time they
clapped that day, but soon the audience and the contestants in particular would learn to clap frequently,
clap often, clap for almost everything. Now they
clapped so Harriet Anderson would continue.

"The very first thing on our agenda today is to
introduce you to some very special women!" The
stage curtains opened all the way, and there stood a
long line of women, also smiling and waving at the
audience. Everyone clapped enthusiastically. It was
immediately obvious they were the old Tri-Rivers

Queens. The audience whispered the news to each other. Maybe the correct name should be "former" Queens, but there they were, a bunch of old Queens wearing glamorous gowns and white satin sashes declaring their title and the year of their reign.

Kate looked up and down the line of smiling, waving old Queens, hoping to see Shirley Mortenson, the woman who gave her the business card that day at the writing club. There she was, wearing a stunning royal blue strapless gown. It fit snugly around her torso down to her hips, where it burst into a full skirt with a train. She also wore the white satin sash from her reign as Ms. Senior Tri-Rivers seven years ago. She would have been 64 years old at that time. Now, at the age of 71, Shirley stood out among the many smiling and waving women, not only because of her vibrant smile but because her strapless gown showed a little cleavage. Somewhere along life's way, hadn't most women been told that ladies of the age of elegance should cover up their arms and cleavage? Apparently that worn-out rule did not apply to these old Queens. Shirley looked fabulous.

With a great hurrah the oldest Queen on the stage was introduced: Eleanor Butler, 87, who had been Ms. Senior Tri-Rivers 25 years ago. She would have been a mere 62 years old then. Her hair was a plain, dull gray, her shoulders stooped, and she used a cane to walk. She didn't bother to wave or smile, she was taking care of the business of walking across the stage. Her Queen's gown was a dark blue chemise, and around her neck she wore a long, graduated pearl necklace. She'd draped a pale gray silk shawl with long silver beaded fringe over her shoulders. Her shoes were sturdy low heels, not the showy high heels worn by the other Queens. She frowned and scowled as she tapped her way across the stage to complete the assemblage of old Queens, seventeen in all. Rapping her cane sternly, she took the very center spot, pushing in between the two tallest old Queens mumbling, "Maybe the two of you can hold me up." As the two tallest Queens stepped apart, one of them put her arm around Eleanor and smiled affectionately.

Each old Queen smiled and introduced herself with her name, age, and city, followed by a recitation of her own thirty second Philosophy of Life. Kate listened closely. They delivered their philosophies with charm and grace, proving it could be done in thirty seconds, amazing as it seemed. Almost every candidate seated in the audience listened carefully and began to scribble notes. Now they had a better understanding of what a Philosophy of Life, as required in the competition, should be. Hearing the old Queens helped to clarify the challenge. When Eleanor Butler, standing in the center, was invited to

introduce herself and give her philosophy, she shook
her head, scowled, and said flatly, "No." Kate decided
Eleanor was a character among the old Queens.
Somehow, her contrariness was amusing, even
charming. The program continued until all seventeen
old Queens had spoken. Then all of them waved and
smiled as the curtains closed.

Harriet Anderson stepped in front of the closed
curtains and greeted the audience again. "Aren't they
just divine in their gowns?" she gushed. Everyone
applauded, their instincts fully inspired by so many
lovely Queens and so many beautiful dresses. Then
she got down to business; it was time to start the information segment of the program. She consulted her
notes.

"Let's begin with gowns. You all need a gown,
and the sooner you get one the better." It was not as
if most of the contestants didn't know, but Harriet
Anderson was in charge, and she was not going to
leave anything unsaid, anything to chance. Then she
continued her introductory talk, moving on to the
next topic. "You will all perform a talent, and you
should already be working on that. And you will
all need to prepare a Philosophy of Life, similar to
those we just heard from our former Queens, which
you must present in thirty seconds." The candidates
nodded knowingly, having received and reviewed
all of their materials before coming here. Then she

reviewed the calendar for the weeks ahead and finally asked questions from the audience. "Anyone?" she invited expectantly. It was hard to imagine what she might have missed, but she looked around the auditorium to see if anyone had a question.

A few rows back a woman raised her hand and stood up. "Myrna Brenner here," she said, smiling brilliantly at Harriet Anderson. "Those dresses the Queens wore?" It was a question, and she continued, "Wow, they were drop dead gorgeous." Everyone applauded. "Where did they find them? And hey, is there any way to get one, you know, used or at a discount or something?"

Who was asking these questions? Everyone craned to see, leaning and turning. Kate recognized her as the woman who was with the man wearing the NY Yankees cap. She was small, but she was definitely one to be noticed. Her flaming red hair was her most dominant feature. Her well-worn skin was living proof of many life experiences, while her clothes were youthful and bold. She was one of those women who may have acquired years, but who refuses to give up a youthful style. She smiled expectantly as she waited for Harriet's answers.

Harriet Anderson returned the smile. "What good questions! The answer is that most Queens buy lots of dresses because they need them for so many occasions. When their closets get full, sometimes they offer their used gowns for sale. We all have to make room for new dresses, I guess!" Everyone chuckled as if they knew exactly what she meant. "A few of the old Queens will have some of their used dresses for sale in the lobby next week. You can check to see if there is one you like." It was a good thing that Myrna asked that question, Kate thought, because she would like to check them out too. She imagined there were other contestants who had similar thoughts.

"Any more questions?" Harriet asked. Hearing none, she moved to the topic of jewelry. "How many of you would be interested in some beautiful jewelry?" A flurry of hands rose. "Great, because I want you to know there will also be jewelry for sale in the lobby next week. Jewelry fit for a Queen. Bling. You know what that is, and that's what we like to call it too. And for those of you who might enjoy a little makeover, a cosmetic specialist will be available for consultations. You can try some new makeup or purchase her products. You will all look very beautiful for the pageant, I promise."

Myrna stood up again, hands on her small hips. "Are we done here?" she wanted to know. Kate muffled a smile at her abruptness.

"Yes, this meeting is adjourned, and I thank you all for coming."

There was a sudden cacophony of excited voices as everyone stood up to exit the auditorium. Myrna hurried out of her row of seats. Her red hair could be seen all the way up the aisle until she exited the auditorium.

In the lobby, several prospective candidates had already lined up at the registration table. The two women working there were volunteers who had competed for Ms. Senior Tri-Rivers in previous years, but had not been selected as winners. Now they offered to help out where they could during the pageant. Today they had volunteered to take registrations. Kate stood in line behind the red-haired woman, Myrna Brenner.

As they waited to sign up, Myrna whispered to her male companion, the man with the Yankees cap. She had one of those voices that never seemed to be soft or quiet, try as she might, and Kate couldn't help but overhear her. Myrna gestured toward the two women volunteers and whispered loudly, "It's very sweet of those ladies to help out this year, but honestly Harold, I don't want to go through all of this and end up like that, just sitting out here taking applications. It must make them feel very bad." Making a sad face, she shook her head and continued to wait in line until it was her turn.

"Hi," said one of the volunteers welcoming Myrna as she stepped forward to the registration desk. "I am so happy to see you are entering the Ms. Senior Tri-Rivers Pageant. Let's just finish up these few things."

Myrna bent over to finish the application and give her money to the volunteer. "We always pay cash," she explained, counting out the $99. Kate stepped to the other end of the table, where the other volunteer was ready to help her complete the forms.

Nearby, two additional volunteers, also former contestants, stood by to welcome candidates after their registration was complete. They introduced themselves as Happy Hookers. "Our job is to assist everyone in the dressing room. We hook, zip, snap, straighten, button and generally help out any way we can. Just holler for a Happy Hooker and one of us will be there!"

Still within hearing distance of Myrna's loud whisper, Kate couldn't help but overhear her comments to her companion once again. "They can have that Happy Hooker job too, Harold," Myrna whispered, shaking her head while she closed her purse. "I won't ever come back if I lose."

He didn't miss a beat. "Don't worry Babe, you won't lose. In my book, you're a winner, and that's that!" They laughed heartily. Kate smiled too.

Hearing them laugh, several women turned around to take a good look at Myrna's companion, Harold. Neither Harold nor Myrna noticed anyone catching a glimpse of them, they were so delighted with each other. Harold was a slight man with narrow shoulders and a small body except for his little pot belly. His wrinkled skin had the look of someone who had smoked a lot over the years, although he wasn't smoking in the "no smoking" area in the lobby. When he smiled, his eyes were lost in wrinkles, and when Myrna spoke, he thrust his head forward to look at her even more adoringly. Raising his NY Yankees baseball hat, he slicked back what remained of his wispy gray hair, which was pulled into a little pony tail secured with a red rubber band. Emblazoned on the front of his gray sweatshirt were the words "I Feel Lucky," a pair of red dice, and the logo of the Three Rivers Casino.

Myrna stood close to him, her arm looped in his. As they walked away from the registration table, Kate thought they could not have been paired any better.

Goodbyes and Hellos

Kate had just finished her registration when she noticed Teresa standing near the auditorium door, buttoning her leather jacket. Her hair bounced freely around her head and shoulders, no longer held back in a clasp. She grabbed a flyaway section of her dark locks and tucked it behind her ear.

Putting away her checkbook and pen, Kate snapped her purse closed as Teresa walk toward her. "Hi Kate," smiled Teresa. "I need to thank these ladies at the registration table before I leave. Do you mind waiting while I do? I'd love to talk to you for a minute." Kate did not mind.

The volunteers at the registration table smiled hopefully at Teresa. Was she going to enter? She smiled back. "Sorry, I don't think I will be able to enter. You know, sometimes things just don't seem right. I am sure everyone will have a great time, and I wish you luck. But for me, I just don't think I can. There are reasons," she said, her voice trailing off. "Mostly, I want to thank you so much for being here. I know everyone appreciates it." The two volunteers smiled and nodded.

Turning to Kate she said, "Thanks for waiting. I wanted to tell you how nice it was to meet you today,

Kate. I want to wish you good luck! Really, you would be a great Queen, representing ladies of The Age of Elegance."

"It was great to meet you, too. I was hoping to see you again, but I understand."

They said goodbye, and with a wave Teresa turned and was out the exit door, high heeled cowboy boots clicking on the pavement as she hurried to her car. Actually it was a big red truck with a side step. In one smooth motion she opened the door and stepped up, slid onto the seat and closed the door. The engine purred with a low diesel rumble as she drove out of the parking lot.

Several other women also exited the building without registering. For whatever reasons, perhaps money or time, this event was not right for them. But as it turned out, fourteen women decided to go with it, and one by one they paid the entry fee, submitted their applications and agreed to the upcoming schedule. The photographer was already taking photos, gliding quietly from one viewpoint to another, snapping informal shots of the new batch of contestants, a process that would continue through-out the weeks ahead. A few women lingered a little longer, chatted with the Happy Hookers and slowly made their way toward the exit.

Sherry Springfield, the pretty blonde lady Kate had noticed earlier, waited by the door, holding the collar of her pale yellow jacket closed at her neck in the cool air. She'd casually put the jacket over her shoulders without actually slipping her arms into the sleeves. Kate had watched Teresa, the woman in cowboy boots, exit through that door just moments ago and now could not help but notice Sherry standing halfway in and halfway out of the door. She looked outside, then inside at the other women chatting in the lobby. Her soft blonde hair framed her face in loose curls.

Sherry noticed Kate and smiled, a pretty smile revealing crinkles around her eyes. "Hi," said Kate, a little embarrassed to be caught staring at her. "Excuse me for staring at you, but I'm a writer and sometimes when I see people like you," she stammered to a halt. "Well, what I am trying to say is, you are just so pretty. Are you going to be in the pageant?" My, Kate did ramble on, or so she thought, reminding herself she really must get her thoughts in order and just stick to introductions.

Sherry looked puzzled. "What?" she said, tilting her head. "Sorry, I didn't quite hear you."

Kate was greatly relieved and moved closer to start again. "I'm Kate Dearborn," she said. "I was just wondering if you are in the pageant."

Sherry seemed to hear the question this time and was pleased at the introduction but demure, her eyes fluttering downward. "Oh, yes, I suppose I am in the pageant now, I am all signed up. I'm waiting for my husband, Danny. He is not too excited about me doing this."

Kate wondered why, but it was not a question she would ask now. "Oh, well, sometimes there are reasons I suppose," she offered.

"Reasons?" laughed Sherry. "Yes, I suppose so, but I went ahead and entered anyway. And I must give my husband credit. He says if it is so important to me, he will support me. He offered to drive me and pick me up, which is great because I don't drive much anymore. So here I am. Oh, my name is Sherry Springfield. I'm from South Mercer."

She looked out the door again. "Oh here he is! Gotta run!" She waved and hurried away. Kate waved back. As she reached the door of the white minivan, Sherry hesitated and turned back. "I'm sorry, did I get your name? What was it?" Kate was sure she had told her, but didn't mind repeating it. Sherry paused, memorizing it. "Yes, Kate. Kate, this is Danny." It was shaded inside the van, and Kate could not see him but waved anyway. "Bye!" they all said.

Tucking her scarf around her neck, Kate left the building too. In the trail of Sherry's hurried departure, Kate thought she noticed a faint floral scent in the air, or was it her imagination. Sherry was as lovely as a flower, thought Kate, a faded flower, still beautiful but without its bloom. Kate, she scoffed at herself, you're getting far too dramatic. If she is a faded flower, then you must be a wilted celery stick. Get in the car and start driving.

She pulled out of the parking lot and turned toward the highway. There was much to think about during the long ride home, including a Philosophy of Life (in thirty seconds, she reminded herself), a talent, and getting a gown. She had many miles to drive before she got to Northridge, where her little doggie would be waiting for her.

$$\sim$$

During the next few days Kate visited another store, an outlet mall, and another thrift store looking for a gown. She found the same thing over and over. Sorry, we don't have gowns. Sorry, nothing in your size. Sorry, only strapless dresses. Sorry, nothing with sleeves. Sorry. Now she began to worry seriously. Finding a gown was not easy, she fretted.

But every time she found herself fretting, she simply had to laugh. How deliciously sweet and funny it all seemed to be fussing and worrying about finding a gown for a pageant. Can you believe it, she asked herself. You are acting like a movie star in Hollywood getting ready for the Academy Awards.

Saturday,
March 15

The First Rehearsal

Kate pulled into the parking lot at the Three Rivers Performing Arts Center. It had been a week since the kick-off meeting, and this morning it was time to get down to business at the first of many Saturday rehearsals. "Please be ready to begin promptly at 8:00 a.m." the instructions read, and here she was with five minutes to spare.

Turning off the engine, she looked around the lot and noticed a big red truck parked down a few spaces. She remembered the pretty lady with the wild dark hair, Teresa, who drove off in a red truck the week before. Kate recalled that at the completion of the kick-off meeting, Teresa had decided not to enter. She said something about an issue, about the pageant not being right for her, about not wearing a gown. That red truck reminded Kate of her, and she wished that she had entered the pageant. Kate would have liked to get to know her better.

She locked the door of her car and walked across the lot, noticing the other cars parked there. There was another truck, an older two-tone teal and white Ford in need of a good wash. It sported a bumper sticker that said "What's not to love about

New York?" Next to it a modest maroon Volkswagen had a "Remember to Support Alzheimer's Research" sticker in the rear window. Kate presumed these were the cars of some of the contestants, and that each of them expressed a personality. Someone drove a big gray van with sliding doors, and someone owned a sky blue Toyota Prius. Kate wondered what clues her own car offered, a three-year-old black Honda Accord, also seriously in need of a good wash. The dirty exterior was evidence that she had driven almost 200 miles in the past week, all over wet and windy highways and byways, just searching for a gown.

Near the far end of the lot was a tan four-door Buick sedan, and next to it was an older BMW 325, a classy car which looked like it had driven many miles but was still going strong. Parked at the very end of the lot, with several spaces between it and the nearest car, was a small silver sports car, shining and spotless with a black convertible top. So sleek and compact was its design, the fenders resembled crouching tigers and the front grill seemed ready to growl. And who does that fearless little beast belong to, wondered Kate. The license plate frame on the sleek silver beast said "Devonville Motors Ltd." Kate looked at it a moment longer before she opened the door to the building.

The Three Rivers Performing Arts Center was the pride of the community, built to serve all the

needs of its arts and performance constituents. Only
ten years old, it was well used throughout the year.
Local school districts used it frequently for music
and drama performances as well as ceremonies such
as high school graduation. A variety of community
groups including drama clubs, dance schools, and
orchestral groups used the center. Community music
groups ranging from choral ensembles to chamber
music and full scale symphony orchestras had their
home on this stage, as did numerous other performing arts organizations and the occasional visiting
musical star or traveling musical and dramatic productions. The Performing Arts Center, with seating
for 1,000 people, served them all.

The stage itself was large enough to accommodate the numerous needs of the various performing
groups. Three floor-to-ceiling curtains were at the
front, the middle, and the back of the stage, each
of them operated separately for various uses. The
side stage areas were large enough to hold huge
props, instruments, chairs, and electrical and sound
equipment for the performers. The sound booth itself
was at the rear of the auditorium, well above the
audience seats.

"Where is the dressing room?" asked the candidates as they entered the building. They wanted to
know where it was so they could hang their coats and
leave their bags. Beginning next weekend they would

use it to change into their gowns and costumes, and for all the other preparation activities, such as hair and makeup.

A volunteer pointed down the hall. "The dressing room is that way. Follow the signs. You can also get to the dressing room directly from the stage," she said. "Just exit at the side of the stage and it's to your right, just down the hall."

Two women greeted them at the door of the dressing room. "Hi, we are your Happy Hookers," said the women as the candidates looked around. "One of us will be here at all times to be sure nothing is disturbed. Feel free to leave any of your belong- ings in the dressing room while you are in rehearsals – your gowns, your coats, whatever else you want to leave here." There were plenty of clothing racks to hang coats, gowns, and costumes, as well as numerous makeup tables with mirrors and great lighting. The contestants hung their coats, unloaded whatever they wished to leave, and made their way to the seats in the auditorium.

The auditorium was laid out in two large pie-shape sections front to back and bisected with two wide aisles side-to-side across the center, making a total of six sections. There were aisles on each side of the auditorium and one aisle down the center. The large center aisle was perfect for graduating students to line up for their diplomas, or for large competing choral or dance groups seated in the audience to access the stage when their turn to perform came or to watch their competition. The central aisle led to the wide set of stairs up to the stage. These stairs made it easy to practice and watch performances during rehearsals, going back and forth from the stage to the seats. This is how the Ms. Senior Tri-Rivers Pageant would use the auditorium during their rehearsals.

The pageant was held in this performing hall every year, and it consistently drew hundreds of people. So popular was the event that ticket sales began early, with blocks of seats sold in advance for family and friends to be seated together. Up to 25 seats could be reserved together in one block, and those tickets typically sold out quickly. General admission seats went on sale after the pre-sales were over but still in plenty of time for everyone to get a good seat. In fact, the auditorium was designed so there was not really a bad seat in the place, just some that were farther back than the others.

While seating throughout the entire auditorium had been open on the first Saturday for the kick-off meeting, today the back sections of the auditorium were closed off with little velvet ropes, and the rear seating area was without lighting. Only the side doors were open for entry. That way, everyone was seated in the front sections, fairly near to the stage.

A few dozen people were seated in the auditorium, eager to see who the new candidates were. Harriet Anderson thought it was a good idea to permit people to watch the rehearsals. She hoped they would talk about it, spread the word. When the final week came, the last rehearsal before the pageant, no one would be allowed to attend the rehearsal, not even husbands, but until then, let them come and enjoy the show in progress. Among those seated in the audience were several former Queens, husbands, friends, helpers, and those few curious people who came to see what was happening. On stage, Harriet Anderson asked everyone to settle down and get ready for the busy morning ahead. And she asked for all of the candidates to move up to the first two rows where it would be easier to get onto the stage, and they could hear her better. All of the candidates picked up the few items they'd kept with them and moved forward.

"Hi Sherry!" Kate said, greeting the pretty blonde lady she'd met in the lobby last weekend. Sherry looked lovely in a flowered dress with soft ruffles down the front. Pale curls framed her face. She did not seem to notice Kate right away as she walked down the auditorium aisle to the front rows, carrying her heavy coat, an umbrella, and a large tote bag. She turned to scoot into the same row as Kate.

When Sherry saw Kate she said with surprise,

"Hi! You're Kate aren't you? Sorry, I was worried I might be late. My husband drove me, but it seemed to take forever. I was so worried when I saw all the other cars were already parked out there."

Kate motioned to the seat next to her. "Come on Sherry, sit with me. You're not late."

Sherry looked around for a place to put her things. Kate gestured at the empty seats in the row. "You can put your things here for now, the rest of us already put ours in the dressing room." Sherry began arranging her coat and other items in the vacant chairs.

"Sorry," Sherry said. "It's a big coat isn't it? It needs a couple of seats." Kate tried again to explain there was a dressing room available, but Sherry was busy arranging the items. When all of the candidates were seated in the designated first two rows, there was still plenty of room to spread out and be comfortable.

Kate looked around. "Teresa!" she called, recognizing the dark-haired woman in the blue jeans who took a seat in the front row, just a couple of seats down from hers. She waved to catch her attention and said, "I noticed a red truck parked outside, and I thought it looked like yours." Last week Teresa had been reluctant to enter, said it just wasn't right for her. But there she was, sitting with the rest of the contestants.

Teresa turned and smiled, "Hi Kate! Great to see you. You look surprised."

Kate nodded. "You must have changed your mind about being in the pageant."

Leaning across the chairs, Teresa explained, "Yes, I changed my mind, and luckily they were still accepting applications, so I entered. Actually, it was my kids, Elena and Miguel, who changed my mind. They are so much like their dad, they can talk me into most anything," she said with a smile. "I had to get up my courage. I needed to feel that this was the right thing for me to do. They are even going to help me find a gown, can you believe that? And my grandson is going to take care of my dogs and horses while I am away on Saturdays. I'll tell you more about it later, I promise." Now that Teresa was here, the number of competitors was fifteen.

Kate looked around to see who else was seated in the first two rows. That was when she saw Marcia Van Horne. A tall, slender woman dressed exquisitely in an icy blue dress and matching jacket, she was hard to miss. Her blunt cut shoulder-length hair was jet black, and her exceptionally pretty face was made up precisely with perfect eyebrows and dusted cheeks. She selected a seat in the very center of the first row, looked around, and leaned over to extend her hand to Teresa. "Hi, I'm Marcia Van Horne. From Devonville." They smiled at each other.

Not wasting a moment, yet in a refined and easy
manner, Marcia turned around to meet Kate, smiled
and offered her hand. Then she turned to Sherry,
who was just finishing arranging her bags, purse,
and coat and did not seem to notice Marcia's gesture.
Marcia just smiled and turned to greet someone else.
She was definitely making her presence known, and
in a most impressive fashion. She oozed elegance.

Marcia Van Horne. Kate repeated the name.
She was undeniably a class unlike most of the contestants, or at least most of the contestants seemed to
see her that way. Not that such elegance intimidated
the other women. The days of being intimidated by
another woman were far behind most of them, and
the chance that this woman could intimidate anyone
who had the courage to enter a pageant for senior
women was pretty slim. No, Marcia Van Horne
was not a class apart because she could intimidate
anyone, but because she definitely awed them. She
breathed elegance, taste, class and – let's face it –
money. Kate had a momentary memory of the silver
sports car parked outside of the auditorium and
would have bet that it belonged to Marcia. Her style
was sleek and smooth, not ruffles and lace. Dancers
and non-dancers alike could see she moved with the
grace of a trained artist. Her jet black hair did not
have a trace of gray, Kate noticed, and she admired
the way it was shiny and free as it brushed her

shoulders and fell over ears adorned with solitaire diamond earrings. The gemstones most certainly had to be real, those women who knew about such things would know. Marcia's tiny wristwatch sparkled on a silver band as if she didn't really need to tell time. The color of her nails, a perfect shade of deep magenta, precisely matched the color of her lips. She was a picture of privilege and perfection.

Why hadn't Kate noticed her before? Surely she would have remembered her from the meeting last week. In time the women would find out that Marcia Van Horne was not at that meeting. She had submitted her application early because of an out-of-town engagement she simply could not miss. Apparently she and her husband had been in Aruba for a weekend wedding. Aruba for a weekend? Such a grand destination for such a short visit punctuated the image of privilege and perfection. Marcia Van Horne was contender number sixteen.

"Hello everyone!" Harriet Anderson was at the podium on the stage. She introduced herself and welcomed everyone to the first rehearsal of the Ms. Senior Tri-Rivers Pageant. Everyone clapped. "Will each of our Ms. Senior Tri-Rivers contestants please stand when I call your name, turn and wave your hand. We want everyone to know who you are." And so it began, sixteen women on a journey to become Ms. Senior Tri-Rivers, the Queen. One by one she called the names. One by one they waved and everyone applauded.

"Before we officially begin the rehearsal, there is one last piece of business. At this time it is my privilege to introduce you to the many others who make this wonderful pageant possible." She named all of them, and they stood too and waved as the audience applauded. Sound and lighting technicians. Stage hands. Prop crew. Happy Hookers. Makeup and wardrobe consultants. Old Queens. She thanked them profusely, reminding the audience that this was the team of people who everyone would work with and depend on during the weeks ahead.

"Now let's get down to business," said Harriet Anderson. And the first order of business was shoes: high heeled shoes.

"Starting today you will wear high heeled shoes during rehearsals, preferably the shoes that you are going to wear in the pageant. Everyone wears high heels. How high is up to you. But loafers, tennis shoes, and saddle shoes are not allowed." Everyone chuckled.

"I hope everyone brought your shoes today. It was mentioned in your materials. Hands up please, did you bring high heeled shoes? Yes? No?" Four contestants did not have their shoes with them. Harriet said she understood that finding the right shoes could be difficult, but she continued, "If you

don't have them yet, be sure to get them, wear them
at home and have them here from now on. Just to be
clear, no flip flops, no mules, no backless sandals. We
don't want to see you fall down because of bad shoes
or high heels you aren't used to. So start wearing
your high heeled shoes today."

Kate's shoes were black pumps without straps,
buckles or ties. They were just plain black leather
with round toes and square heels, but not too high.

They were her "go to" shoes for many occasions.
This morning she'd dressed in tailored black slacks
and a khaki sweater and brown leather boots, but she
tucked her black shoes into her purse and changed
into them in the dressing room. She was used to
wearing the black shoes to meetings or to the theatre
and didn't expect it to be any different during the
pageant. One less item to worry about, was how she
thought of it. They were the shoes she would wear
throughout the pageant.

However, seated at the very end of the row, next
to the center aisle, Anita Archer laughed cheerfully,
raised her hand and said, "This is going to be interesting. I haven't worn high heels since high school.
I'm wearing my sandals today, but I promise to have
high heels next week."

"Let's get started," said Harriet Anderson.
"All of you lovely contestants will come up the
center aisle, up the stairs, and onto the stage. Go

all the way to the back curtain and line up in front
of it. Each of you will take your turn and walk up
to the microphone and tell us your Philosophy of
Life. Remember, it can only be thirty seconds long.
Philosophy of Life was on your schedule for this
week."

In the last few days, Kate wrote several versions
of her philosophy of life. She wrote them by hand to
begin with, entered them on the computer, printed
them, scribbled down notes, crossed things out,
deleted, retyped, and crossed out over again as she
tried to come up with thirty seconds of ideas that
did not sound insincere or silly. Today each contestant would present their Philosophy of Life for the
first time no matter how rough or what state it was
in. Kate reached inside her purse and pulled out the
neatly folded paper containing her philosophy. She
was prepared, although she was not confident about
what she had written.

Harriet Anderson asked who was ready. "Hands
up, everyone. Yes?"' All hands went up. Most of the
women clutched sheets of paper and planned to read
theirs. Some had already memorized theirs, obvious
by their empty hands. Lowering their hands, all the
contestants began scooting across the row of seats to
the center aisle and waited there for Harriet's signal
to go up the stairs to the stage.

Anita Archer, the woman who hadn't worn

high heels since high school was the first in line at the bottom of the steps to the stage, holding her written notes in her left hand. Aware of the contestants waiting behind her, she hurried up the steps not bothering to grasp the handrail with her right hand. Her flowery, loose dress fluttered around her ankles and suddenly her skirt caught in her slip-on sandals and she lurched forward in a sliding fall, landing by the podium where Harriet Anderson stood. There were a few shrieks and several people rushed forward to help her.

In the commotion, Harriet Anderson leaned over and extended her hand. "Anita! Are you okay? Are you okay?"

Slowly, Anita rolled to her side, waited, then sat up and smiled at everyone, "I'm okay. It's these sandals." Almost 5' 10" tall, she stretched out her long legs and wiggled her feet, sandals still attached. "See – there is a reason you're not supposed to wear them. I'd rather fall today than on stage on the day of the pageant. No more sandals, I promise."

Brushing her long hair aside, she took the outstretched hand of Harriet Anderson and stood up, smiling and waving as if she had just performed a stunt. From the audience came a whistle and a shout, "Atta girl, Anita! That's my girl!" It was Anita's husband, Mr. Nick. He would become a regular fixture in the audience, always there to cheer on his wife.

Anita waved back at him, "Thanks, Mr. Nick!" With that, she straightened her dress and continued to the back of the stage.

When the candidates were lined up, Harriet Anderson explained what they would do next. "For the time being you will stand in front of this curtain, but on the night of the pageant you will stand behind it. Now I want you to line up in alphabetical order by last name. That will be the order I will use to call you for your Philosophy of Life. And be careful, please, no more falls today."

They bustled around, sorting out the alphabetical order by last name. Up until now no one had paid much attention to last names, but suddenly it was important.

"A? Who has a last name starting in A?"

Anita raised her hand and waved, "Here! My name is Archer, Anita Archer." She took her place at the front of the line, followed by Olga Asamova, and so on until everyone was in line alphabetically, A to Z. Angeline Zolta was the last in line.

Alphabetical Order by Last Name
    Anita Archer
    Olga Asamova
    Myrna Brenner
    Judith Ann Cole
    Kate Dearborn

Bonnie Gabriel
Stephanie McCoy
Sandi Meredith
Jane Morrison
Helen Nicholas
Rosemarie North
Carol Parcellia
Teresa Rodriguez
Sherry Springfield
Marcia Van Horne
Angeline Zolta

"Is everyone ready?" Harriet Anderson asked, and everyone nodded.

"You will walk from the back of the stage to the microphone near the front of the stage." Counting the steps aloud as she demonstrated, it was about twenty paces. "It may seem like a mile the first few times but you will get used to it. Once you are at the microphone, you will introduce yourself giving your name, age and city. Nothing else. Name. Age. City. After you say these three things, just stand still – smile at the audience – and wait for them to applaud.

"You have thirty seconds to give your Philosophy of Life. When does that begin?" She gestured to two women seated at a table at the side of the stage. "My assistants, these two former Queens, are the timekeepers today. They each have a stop watch to keep the exact time of your philosophy. The time will begin at the moment of your first word. Not your name. Not your age. Not your city. The first word of your Philosophy of Life. They will stop the watch when you are finished. There are two assistants so they can compare their times and be sure they are accurate. They will write down the number of seconds on an index card and hold it up for me to read aloud. Remember, you are aiming for thirty seconds. Any questions?

"All right then, let's get started."

Philosophies and Other Words

When Shirley first urged Kate to participate in the Ms. Senior Tri-Rivers Pageant, she predicted there would be great writing topics. Now that Kate was surrounded by the women of the pageant she thought about seizing that opportunity. After all, it was one of the reasons she had decided to participate. With all of the candidates assembled on the stage of the Performing Arts Center, she wondered if she could describe each of them in one word. First impression words, she would call them. That would be a good start for writing about them, she thought.

Anita Archer walked to the microphone. "Anita Archer. 68. Colby." She turned her head to Harriet and asked, "Is that right?"

Harriet nodded, "Yes, that's right. Start again, please, without asking if it is right. Go back to the curtain, walk forward, speak, then wait for the audience to applaud."

Anita started over. "Anita Archer. 68. Colby." She paused for the applause, then continued. "I believe the most important thing I can do in life is be a good wife to my husband and a good mother to my five sons. These days I also add the honor of being a

good grandmother to my ten grandchildren. Life can
be filled with joy, but it is not always easy, and these
three jobs are the most challenging in God's universe.
Therefore, my philosophy is to do my best to be a
good person, a good example, and a good servant of
God, living as He has showed us so that we might all
know his Kingdom."

The assistant raised the card so that Harriet
could read the number of seconds. "Thirty three
seconds, Anita," said Harriet Anderson. "Very good.
Just take out a few words or speak just a little
faster and you'll bring it down to the required thirty
seconds. For now, please take your place at the end
of the line. We will go through the whole thing again
after everyone is finished."

Kate thought about a good word to describe
Anita Archer. Surprised, she found she could think
of several. Her objective with her word game was to
think of just one. Kate decided she would describe
Anita as Motherly.

Olga Asamova was second. She walked to
the microphone and looked at the audience with
great assurance. Observing her, Kate thought she
was either a natural born speaker or had done this
before. She knew the word for her: Confident. Kate
was confident she had chosen the right word as she
listened to Olga speak.

"Olga Asamova. 64. Mercer City. As a teacher,
I know how important self-esteem is to a student's

success. If this is true for students in the small and protected setting of a school classroom, it is also true for each of us in the much larger setting of our own lives. We must know our own self-worth, our own strengths, our own standards, our own spiritual beliefs. We must stand up for ourselves, and we must be strong enough to stand beside others when they need us. My philosophy of life is to believe in yourself and never be afraid to do what is right."

Myrna Brenner was third. Myrna wore thigh-high black patent leather platform boots with a short red skirt and a black turtle neck sweater. Kate found it easy to choose a word to describe her. Attitude. My oh my, thought Kate, she has Attitude.

"Myrna Brenner. 75. Northridge. My philosophy of life is simple. You only go around once, so enjoy the sun when it shines, don't get soaked when it rains, and bundle up when it snows. Don't be afraid to cry when life gets tough, but don't go making trouble for yourself. Mostly, life is good, so get out and grab the good stuff! Smile and laugh a lot. Smell the flowers and shoot for the moon. That's my philosophy."

Myrna winked at someone in the audience when she finished. Kate wondered if Harriet Anderson noticed, and if she did would she say something. Instead, Harriet seemed oblivious. After all, the man in the NY Yankees cap, the smiling recipient of

Myrna's wink, was clearly her supporter and perhaps Harriet Anderson appreciated that.

Kate turned her attention to the next competitor, Judith Ann Cole. As she walked carefully to the microphone, she had a pronounced limp and leaned heavily on a cane for support. Her black shoes had sturdy, one-piece soles that were about one inch thick in front and two inches high in back. Noticing she wore simple and modest attire, unadorned hair, and no makeup, Kate's one word impression for Judith Ann: Earnest.

"Judith Ann Cole. 68. Clarksdale. I have always lived to honor God, and my philosophy of life has never changed. I have been a survivor of many things in my life, including a debilitating back injury, financial loss, and the death of a child. Nothing is more heartbreaking than the loss of a child, and yet with God's help, His guidance and care, I have lived through these things and carry on with life. I am a wife and a mother and I live to sing His praises. I am taking part in this pageant to share His word, which is my philosophy of life."

Kate was fifth. As she walked the twenty paces to the microphone, she was surprised at how nervous she was. This certainly was not the first time she'd ever stood before an audience, yet her hands shook and her breath felt short. Panicky, she thought, that's how to describe me in one word.

"Kate Dearborn. 73. Northridge," she began, but she was so nervous she forgot to pause and rushed right into her philosophy. "Life goes by quickly . . ."

Harriet Anderson interrupted. "No, Kate. You need to pause, wait. Please go back to the curtains and start over." And she did. Clutching her notes in her hand, she began again.

"Kate Dearborn. 73. Northridge." She paused. This time she got it right. "Life goes by quickly. When you are young, you think you know what you want from life, and you make your choices. Time goes by, and you learn that maybe those choices were not the best. But what is done is done, and you cannot go back and do it over. My philosophy is to look carefully at the choices I have now and to imagine the possibilities that lie ahead. We do not know how much time there is, so we must be careful with every moment. As Emily said in *Our Town*, "Do any human beings ever realize life while they live it – every, every minute?' My philosophy is to do that now."

To Kate, the concept was right but the words were not. She was unhappy with her first try, and not just because her voice was shaky. She already knew the words she had written were not refined into what she wanted them to be. Vowing to herself to review and refine it again, she hurried to the back of the line at the rear of the stage.

"That was thirty-seven seconds. Cut it down, and memorize, Kate, memorize," reminded Harriet Anderson. Kate nodded. She was already making revisions in her head.

The alphabetized list continued. Bonnie Gabriel was next. Swagger, thought Kate. That would be the single word I would use to describe her.

"Bonnie Gabriel. 64. Pendleton. My philosophy is that life is a not a cake walk, and I am a baker so I would know. You could say it's not a laughing matter, but it can be. If you think you can always bake a nice cake, think again. My philosophy is to plan the way I want things to go but not to expect them to always turn out. Like baking a cake, you get ingredients, measure them, mix them, put them in a pan, and bake them. Even when you do everything right, the cake may fall flat. So does life sometimes. My philosophy is to do my best, to fix what I can, and to laugh if I have to and move along."

Clearly frustrated, Harriet Anderson held up Bonnie's time card. "Thirty eight seconds, Bonnie. You need to cut it way back." Without any touch of swagger, Bonnie nodded.

Harriet turned to all of the contestants who were lined up at the back of the stage. "You must cut these down to thirty seconds. May I share a method for getting your philosophy to exactly thirty seconds?"

They nodded their heads, yes. They were eager

to hear. Most were well aware that their philosophies were too long. It was a frequent complaint
and concern. Most had tried using the second hand
on their wristwatch. Digital watches were not very
useful. They had not found a very satisfactory
method for timing themselves.

"I wish I had mentioned this earlier, but here's
one way to time yourself," said Harriet. "Go to your
kitchen. Stand in front of your microwave. Set the
timer for thirty seconds. Read your philosophy in
front of your microwave and check the time. Adjust
until you get the right amount of time. It really
works. Remember, the judges will deduct points
if your philosophy is too long. So ladies, use your
microwave to cut down your Philosophy of Life to
thirty seconds!"

The idea of reciting to the microwave made
everyone smile. The contestants made a mental note:
Philosophy of Life in front of microwave.

Next was Stephanie McCoy. Watching her
approach the microphone, Kate chose the word
Straightforward. She recalled how businesslike she
had been the morning when she entered the auditorium with her friend, Rosemarie. Now she was quite
purposeful as she spoke. When Stephanie finished
her philosophy, Kate thought her word choice was
good.

"Stephanie McCoy. 66. Pendleton. My philosophy is to be mindful of all the blessings I have and

proceed with kindness. Don't lash out in anger, don't be vindictive, and don't carry a grudge. Instead, think of ways to be gentle and helpful. Don't be afraid of giving unconditional love, or of receiving it. Be kind and caring to those around you, be kind to all creatures large and small, and be kind to this beautiful green earth we live on. And most of all, remember that you are only human: be kind to yourself. "

Now it was Sandi Meredith's turn. Kate had noticed that Sandi Meredith was always there ahead of the others, seated up in the front row, ready to begin. Kate chose the word Reliable for her.

"Sandi Meredith. 62. East Mercer City. In my life I have enjoyed good health, good friends, a good family. I've had many opportunities to love and be loved, to give and to receive. When I was young I took them as they came along, and sometimes I just walked on without looking back. It's not the best way to do things. My philosophy today is to be grateful for what I receive each day, to give in return, and don't burn bridges as I go along because someday I may have to walk back over them. Be good to others, and they will be good to you."

As Jane Morrison went to the front of the stage, Kate watched her smile. She had a relaxed and easy manner. Something in her face made Kate describe her as Fun.

"Jane Morrison. 63. Mercer City. When I look back on my life, I don't want to have any regrets. I know I have made mistakes, but I also have done some really good things. I know I have not been perfect, but I also tried hard to be my best. I don't want to wish I had done something, but didn't. I want to live life to the fullest, and when I die I want to be thoroughly used up, out of breath, and shouting, Wow, what a ride! I rejoice in life, and if it is just a brief candle, then I want to make it burn as brightly as possible before it goes out."

Next was Helen Nicholas. Serious and serene, she moved with poise to the microphone. Helen is beautiful, thought Kate, and that is the word I will use for her: Beautiful.

"Helen Nicholas. 71. Three Points. God put us here for a reason. We may not understand it, but whether we are paupers or royals, scholars or dolts we are part of His plan. I believe we are tested throughout our lives. My philosophy is to accept God's plan with dignity and diligence; to do what I am called to do; to be an example of God's grace through all things. I believe each day is a gift, and we must accept not only the good but the difficult and sad. I believe God put me here, in this pageant, at this very moment, so that you will know that no matter how difficult your burden may be, you too can go on."

Rosemarie North was very easy for Kate to describe in one word. As Rosemarie took over the stage with great posturing and flair, it was obvious the word must be Dramatic.

"Rosemarie North. 69. Pendleton. Life is so beautiful! I wake up every morning and wonder what wonderful things will happen today. I believe if I look for the good things in life I will find them. And to be sure things are good, I share my smile with everyone I meet. I am smiling at all of you now! You have probably heard my philosophy of life before: don't worry, be happy! And remember, in a pageant – or anywhere – there is no beauty like happiness!"

Looking at Carol Parcellia, Kate liked her no nonsense way of getting to the microphone and stating her philosophy. Stable. Kate chose that word for her.

"Carol Parcellia. 64 Mercer City. I live my life by the Golden Rule, which is to do unto others as you would have them do unto you. I believe in a code of ethics which includes my personal behavior and my professional actions. In my personal relationships, living by the Golden Rule means respect, appreciation and love. As a pediatric nurse, the Golden Rule means treating my patients with dignity and kindness. My philosophy is to live by the Golden Rule, doing my best in all things, and hoping I will get the same in return."

And then there was Teresa. Kate already knew a lot about her but had not been able to pick just one word for her. One word, she pondered. Although Kate thought perhaps the word Committed described her, she suddenly thought of another word: Devoted. It wasn't quite the right word either. Kate decided she would wait to choose just the right word for her new friend. Something told her a better word could be found.

"Teresa Rodriguez. 61. Grover Plains. Love is the most important thing in life. Without love, the world can be a hollow place. Being deeply loved by someone gives you strength, while loving someone deeply gives you courage. My philosophy is to believe in the wonder of love and give and receive it whenever I can."

When Teresa was finished, Harriet Anderson said, "It's only about twenty seconds, Teresa. Is there anything you would like to add? You have a few more seconds."

Teresa did not pause to think about her reply. "No," she said, "that is exactly how I feel and everything I want to say."

Kate realized that although Harriet questioned the length of some of the philosophies, she did not critique the content. Harriet was wise, Kate recognized as the morning unfolded. She does not critique a philosophy of life because each one is personal and unique. Teresa had just shared her most personal thoughts. Twenty seconds was all the time she needed. There really was nothing more for her to say.

Sherry Springfield was next. Kate noticed Carol gently nudge her, saying, "Sherry? It's your turn." Sherry looked at Carol and seemed uncertain for just a moment before she walked to the microphone.

Delicate. Kate wondered if that word best described her. She knew Sherry, and yet she did not know her at all it seemed. There was something about Sherry that was still too unknown. For now she would stick with Delicate.

"Sherry Springfield. 66. South Mercer City. When I was a girl, I thought the most important thing was to be pretty. Everyone liked a pretty girl. But as I grew older I saw there were lots of pretty girls, and that beauty alone was not what made them happy. I believe we should all find something to share that contributes to making the world a better place. That is what makes us happy. I have found I can share music, especially through song, and flowers, especially the roses I grow myself. I believe that each of us is as beautiful as what we share with others. That is my philosophy of life."

When Marcia stepped forward, Kate did not have to ponder how to describe her. To Kate, Marcia was a very big presence. She was beautiful, poised and prepared. Words such as Dynamic and Forceful described her, but for some reason Kate chose another word: Disciplined.

Marcia lightly brushed the front of her dress to smooth out any wrinkles, and walked elegantly to the front of the stage. She smiled and looked at the audience, her voice strong and confident.

"Marcia Van Horne. 63. Devonville. I believe that life is what you make it as long as you do your best and set your sights high. The world is filled with opportunities, almost anything is possible for those who dream big and work hard. If I had not learned these things, I could not have controlled my own destiny, succeeded in my career, served on the Modern Art Museum Auxiliary Board, and prepared to stand here in my quest to be Queen. Believe in who you are and in what you can do. That is my philosophy."

Harriet smiled with enthusiasm. "That was exactly thirty seconds! Thank you Marcia," she said, beaming because somebody finally got it right. Marcia turned with assurance and walked back to the line of candidates.

"Woo Woo, Devonville. Isn't that the fancy place for rich people?" whispered Myrna, but her whisper was still loud enough to be heard by everyone. Harriet Anderson heard her and gave her a stern glance.

"Sorry," whispered Myrna, turning to Marcia, "I

didn't mean to be rude." Marcia nodded.

Angeline Zolta was the final candidate in alphabetical order. Kate tried to limit herself to just one
word. It was not easy, when it came to Angeline.
Kate, she said to herself, this is your word game and
you can choose more than one first impression word
if you want. So Kate chose two words: Strong and
Elegant. They both suited Angeline so well. Kate
was enchanted as Angeline walked to the front of the
stage, seeming to savor each step. Angeline spoke
with a slight accent. Kate could not identify where it
was from, but soon learned.

"Angeline Zolta. 66. Pendleton. Ever since I was
a little girl in South Africa I dreamed of the things
I wanted in my life. I believe a dream can become
a goal, and if you truly understand it you can make
plans to reach that goal. I am not so silly to think that
every dream can come true, but if you don't give it a
try, how will you know? My philosophy of life is to
listen to my heart, hear my dreams and make them
my goals so that they can come true."

It was 10:45 a.m. when the Philosophy of Life
rehearsal ended. With what Kate thought might be
a sigh of relief, Harriet Anderson said, "Thank you,
ladies, you were wonderful. That concludes this
portion of our rehearsal. Let's take a break."

∼

What had seemed like it would be simple enough had

turned out to be not so easy. Several women were not satisfied with what they had prepared, and also realized they had some serious editing to do in order to meet the thirty second time limit. Nonetheless, that part of the first rehearsal was behind them and they had an understanding of how it would go the night of the pageant.

Bonnie took her cup of coffee and joined some of the women as they waited in their seats for the next instructions, the next activity. "I'm exhausted already and we've hardly started," she moaned. "And I'll tell you this – if I said what was really on my mind, if I told you all my real philosophy of life I'd probably be thrown outta here in exactly thirty seconds, which happens to be the exact time we have to speak." She was on a roll and the rest of the women were ready to hear what she had to say. "My real philosophy is to never get married because there ain't gonna be no happily ever after. I know. I was married once. My husband was such a jerk." She raised a finger, like a teacher pointing to a word, "Correction. He is such a jerk. And he is my ex-husband. Ex," she emphasized.

As a comedian, Bonnie was funnier even than the character she would portray as her talent, Mildred. Bonnie couldn't resist telling funny tales of how inept her husband was around the house. "He couldn't change a light bulb. Guess there wasn't one in his head either. He was a natural born idiot."

About his other activities she was sarcastic and even bitter. "Conveniently, he couldn't remember where he had been when he didn't come home some nights, and he never did learn to stop saying some girl's name in his sleep." When it came to being a contestant for Ms. Senior Tri-Rivers, she was delighted. "I just love being in the Ms. Senior Tri-Rivers competition. He and I were both 19 when we got married. Same age exactly. So do the math: we were both 19 then, we are both 64 now. When he sees me wearing a crown like an old Queen, it will remind him of how old he really is."

Everyone was laughing when Bonnie quipped with a smile, "Time's up! Look alive gang! Harriet Anderson has our latest orders." It was almost 11:15 a.m. when everyone's attention turned back to the stage.

"Well ladies, how is everyone doing?" asked Harriet Anderson, who had perked up somewhat after the break. Everyone clapped, of course. "And how do you like all the smiling today?" She smiled at the women and they smiled back. It was true, they had been expected to smile most of the morning, and some smiled more than they ever smiled in a week.

They had been told over and over to smile when you say your name. Smile when you say your age. Smile when you say your city. Smile when you begin your philosophy, smile in the middle, smile when you are finished. Smile even if your cheeks hurt from smiling.

Now she directed everyone to line up on the stage one more time so the photographer could take a picture of the very first day of rehearsal. "This is not a formal portrait. We just want you to gather together in a relaxed pose so Dave can get everyone in the photograph. And smile ladies, smile!" They all smiled. Click-click-click and the photographer was finished. The record of the first day of rehearsals was in the can, as they used to say. More likely, it was digital.

"Great job, everyone, but you are not quite finished." There was a murmur of disappointment among the contestants. "Please return to the dressing room. Yes, the dressing room. It is 11:15 a.m. now. At 11:30 a.m. I expect everyone to be lined up on the side stage in performance order."

There was a buzz among the contestants. Performance order? Was that the order in which they were going to perform? Anticipating the questions, Harriet went on to explain. "Good, I got your attention. The list has been posted in the dressing room. Just find your spot in the performance order and be ready whenever you are asked to line up that way.

"This will be the last thing we do today. We want you to get used to checking the dressing room for your performance order and other information. As soon as you know your spot in the order, you can pick up your coat and other items and come back to the side stage and line up. This will be your first look at our performance order for the pageant, and the last thing we will do today. Thank you. "

Sherry gathered up her coat and other items from the chair. "I was wondering about where to change," she said to Kate. "Can I follow you to the dressing room?" Together, they walked up the stairs to the stage, then out the side door.

"This is the easiest way to get to and from the stage," Kate explained as they made their way across the stage and out the side exit. Little did either Kate or Sherry know how frequently they would walk this way in the weeks ahead.

Hair, the Crowning Glory

On a bright Tuesday morning, Kevin touched up
Kate's makeup. It had been more than two weeks
since Kate first visited the salon. As he waved the big
fluffy brush in his right hand he declared to Shirley,
"The new makeup, the eyebrows, they definitely
help."

"Her face looks so much better," Shirley agreed.
Kate suppressed a laugh. Here they were again,
talking about her as if she was not there.

Kate had quickly grown accustomed to the
new makeup and actually liked her new look. Lately
when she looked at herself in the mirror she began
to think a new hairstyle might also be an improve-
ment. She may have been reluctant before, but now
she looked forward to a change. Not a big change,
but something new. She could use a little help from
Kevin.

"I'd love to go with you," said Shirley Mortenson
when Kate mentioned it to her. "If he has an opening,
let's go see him on Tuesday."

And that is how they came to be there at 10:00
a.m. that morning. "Over here," he said, extending
his arm toward the chair. Kate sat down and Kevin

fastened a lavender bib around her neck. Turning
the chair so she faced the mirror, he stood behind her
with Shirley at his side. The three of them – Kate,
Kevin and Shirley - stared at her reflection. Kate
wondered what they were thinking.

Cupping his hand over his face he whispered to
Shirley, "I'm not sure what we can do with her hair!"
He swept back his own blond tipped locks as if to
emphasize what a head of hair should look like.

Shirley cupped her hand and explained to Kevin
in similar hushed tones, "We just talked about doing
a little update, nothing drastic."

Kate still stared straight ahead at her reflection,
noting that her hair looked like it always did, a simple
style, parted on the side and turned under in a little
pageboy. Kevin touched her hair very lightly, as if
testing it. He cleared his throat.

"So, Kate," he said in a normal talking voice,
"what are we going to do today? Just a little off here
and there?"

Kate blinked. He was talking to her! "Yes," she
said, "just a little."

He cupped his hand and whispered to Shirley
again. "We simply must ask her about changing her
hair color before we style it. It definitely needs some
pop."

Hair color? Uh oh, Kate thought. That was not
in her plans. It was something Kate experimented

with a few years ago when gray began to appear
here and there in her brown hair. She bought some
do-it-yourself color at Drug-Mart one afternoon. It
came in a box with a photo of a woman with shining,
smooth, rich chestnut brown hair. Kate unfolded the
page of directions and read them carefully. Twice.
She took the small bottle of clear dark liquid and
carefully added it to the big bottle of white lotion.
"Mix well" said the instructions, so she shook it
vigorously. Draping a towel around her neck and
donning the latex gloves that came with the instructions, she carefully made a part down the center
of her head and squeezed the mixture along it. For
the next few minutes she parted the rest of her hair
and applied the thick concoction all over her head.
The gooey mix slowly turned dark yellow while she
waited forty minutes, per the instructions. When the
timer rang, she rushed to the shower.

As she washed out the lotion the water turned
brown, and it flowed down the drain. When it finally
ran clear, she squeezed the moisture from her hair
and stepped out of the shower. She pulled on her
bathrobe, and hurried to the mirror. Yes. Her hair
was brown. Rubbing it vigorously with the towel
and turning the hairdryer on high, it was dry in ten
minutes. She was shocked. Her hair had turned a
very dark brown, as brown as the picture on the box.
Not a speck of gray remained. But it didn't look like

the model. To Kate it looked exactly like she had dunked her head in a jar of shoe polish. Shoe polish! It took six weeks for it to fade out.

"I'd rather just keep my own color," she said when Kevin presented a card of samples and photos of various hair colors. She dreaded Kevin's reaction but continued, "I don't mind the gray, there's not that much, yet." He gasped and looked away as if it was too much for him to bear. Clearly she had no clue about what a good color makeover could do, at least according to his body language. His shoulders slumped as Shirley and Kate watched him leave the room.

"Now what?" Kate asked, very concerned.

"Wait," reassured Shirley. "He'll be back." Shirley relaxed, looked in the mirror and primped her own hair. Apparently she had been through this with Kevin before.

In a few minutes he returned with a small spray bottle filled with water, and pair of very short scissors. He began snipping a little bit here and a little bit there. Snip by snip Kate's hairstyle was transformed. No longer the plain little pageboy, it gradually became a looser, fuller style. He held the spray bottle in one hand and misted her hair, using his other hand to fluff, squeeze and ruffle it. "Just use your hands," he said in stern tones. "Your hair should never ever see a hairdryer." He put down the spray bottle so he could use both hands. "Move it like this and toss it around wild and free."

For a moment he reminded her of a mad magician, hands swirling through her newly snipped locks. Suddenly, with a grand gesture he threw his arms out wide, reached for a large gold and black can, and sprayed a fine mist of Crowning Glory over Kate's tousled locks. "Just so it won't frizz," he whispered as he set it down. While Kate did not exactly consider herself the wild and free type, she liked the idea of such effortless style and the fact that she suddenly looked much more – she searched for a word to describe her new look but couldn't find one. She, the wordsmith, was momentarily at a loss for words? In any case, it was thrilling, she had to admit.

Shirley was ecstatic. Admiring Kate's misted and tousled locks, she cried, "Wonderful! Fabulous! Kevin you are a genius!" Kate wished she had thought to say that when she was at a loss for words a moment ago, but it was too late now except for her to echo Shirley.

"Wonderful! Fabulous!" echoed Kate. That was all it took for Kevin to remove the lavender bib, then whirl her chair this way and that way so she could see the whole effect, front, side and back.

"Yes," he sighed, clearly exhausted from all he had been through, but smiling.

Shirley picked up her coat from a chair. She

kissed Kevin on the cheek and gave Kate a hug. "I
have to run, but wasn't this just marvelous? Kevin,
you are the best! See you on Saturday, Kate." She
hurried out the door while Kate finished up with
Kevin.

He pulled a little wireless tablet from his apron
and began to calculate his fees. "No charge for color,
of course" he sniffed. He handed the tablet to her.
The total was in big numbers on the little screen.
Kate's eyes widened just a bit as she wondered what
to do now. "Just use your finger to sign. Right here."
She smiled to herself at this marvelous technology.
After all she still used a paper calendar, so this was
really a reminder of her 'age of elegance.' Moving her
fingertip across the little screen, she signed her name.

A receipt emerged from a nearby printer. He
handed it to her and asked, "Shall I email this to you
too?"

"No thanks," said Kate as she tucked the receipt
into her purse.

He handed her a small silver bag with ribbon
handles. "These are some samples of conditioner for
plain hair, no color," he sniffed. "Enjoy!"

They walked to the door and he held it open for
her. "Bye bye!" he waved. "And good luck!"

Kate tousled her hair with her fingers before
waving back to him. "Thanks Kevin. See you again!"
And she meant it.

Saturday,
March 22

Costumes and Talent

Posted on the dressing room door was the large list titled Performance Order. It was the same one that had been posted the previous Saturday. Everyone took another look at it as they entered.

PERFORMANCE ORDER

1. Anita Archer - piano solo
   "Piano Roll Blues"

2. Stephanie McCoy - modern dance
   "Pink Panther"

3. Judith Ann Cole – singer
   "I Saw the Way"

4. Olga Asamova – clogging dance
   "Mountain Music"

5. Angeline Zolta – singer
   "Unforgettable"

6. Carol Parcellia - Tahitian dance
   "Ua Tai Au Ia Oe-Aparima"

7. Teresa Rodriguez - singer
   "They Were You"

8. Bonnie Gabriel - comedian
   Mildred

9. Helen Nicholas - singer
   "Sunrise, Sunset"

10. Kate Dearborn – poetry
    Two poems by Robert Frost
11. Jane Morrison - interpretative dance
    "The Way You Make Me Feel"
12. Myrna Brenner – singer
    "New York, New York"
13. Sandi Meredith - magician
    Dinner Table Magic
14. Sherry Springfield – singer
    "Shall We Dance?"
15. Rosemarie North – actress soliloquy
    Hamlet/Ophelia
16. Marcia Van Horne - jazz dance
    "All That Jazz"

"It's been a week since we saw it but it still says I am number 1," smiled Anita. "I think that is a good omen."

Olga was pleased to be number 4. Bonnie liked being in the middle of the pack at number 8. "Oh good," sighed Sherry, "I am not until number 14, so I will have plenty of time to change."

Marcia was number 16. "I like being last," she said with cool satisfaction.

The morning began with a greeting from Harriet Anderson. "We can't wait to see your performances and costumes today. Once again I remind you, the time limit is two-and-a-half minutes. If your act runs longer we will warn you and ask you to make adjustments.

"Today, we will also evaluate your costume to be sure it is appropriate for an event like ours. This is a family show, need I say more?"

She paused, then continued. Apparently she felt she needed to say more. "We will take a look to see if your costume needs any sort of adjustment. What kind of adjustment? An example might be when a dress is too long and presents a tripping hazard. We will ask you to shorten it. Or if you are wearing a hat or a mask which interferes with your vision, we will ask you to change that.

"Others adjustments might be when two people wear nearly identical costumes. We will ask the two of you get together and work it out. One year we had nearly identical clown outfits. Seems the local clown store had a clearance sale or something. We can't forget the *Phantom of the Opera* half-mask that was glued on. Our contestant didn't want it to come off during her performance. It didn't, but it would not come off afterwards either.

"Then there is the subject of modesty. Sometimes a dress or top is very tight, causing a bounteous bosom to simply burst over the top or even out the sides like ripe fruit, if you will excuse my scandalous metaphor. While we all appreciate ripe fruit, this pageant is a family show and we prefer you to keep

the fruit beneath your clothing." This brought a howl
of laughter, followed by cheers when she offered to
go on.

"We also discourage sky high heels or stilts
which might break an ankle if you should trip or fall,
head attire that sheds copious amounts of feathers, or
props such as whipped cream or bubbles, which can
land on the stage creating slippery surfaces.

"But the number one offender is. . ." and she
paused before finishing the sentence. "Are you ready
for this?" she asked. "The number one offender is
jiggles and wiggles. Wiggly thighs and tummies are
simply not attractive bathed in the lights of the stage,
and when we notice these, we ask you to pull on
a tight and firm undergarment. If you are already
wearing one of those elastic wonders, we ask you to
wear two. And there you are, that is your costume
approval adventure." Everyone clapped in delight.

Today the technical aspects of sound and
lighting would also be checked, including microphones, spot lights, and props. Everything had to be
satisfactory. It would be a busy morning.

In the dressing room, Kate was the first person
changed into her talent costume. She wore a knee-
length gray dress with short sleeves and a round
neck. "I can't think of anything better to wear for
a poetry reading," she had explained to her sister
during a phone call. "It needs to be simple. Even the

poet laureate just wears a plain suit and tie." With her plain dress she wore a simple string of pearls and her black shoes.

"Is that your costume?" asked one of the Happy Hookers. She added, with a smile, "It's not going to be a lot of work for us, is it?"

As Kate reviewed the performance list, Myrna Brenner joined her. Myrna's flaming red hair was newly chopped into a short spikey cut and she had put some sort of gel in it to make it stand on end. She had not dressed yet and wore only her under- garments, a bright green bra and panties. She was chatty, saying, "Looks like I'm number 12, at least I'm not lucky number 13. Get it? Number 13 does the magic, good luck on that!" she laughed.

"Hey," she said to Kate, "last week at rehearsal didn't I hear you say you're from Northridge? I'm from Northridge too. Just been there about a year. It's a very nice place to retire. Not like New York, but nothing is like New York, you know? Imagine both of us from the same little town." She shook her head as if it was an amazing coincidence.

"Honey, I want you to know when I heard you say Northridge was your town, the first thing I thought about was carpooling, you know, sharing a ride from there since we are both coming this way, and I would really love to do that, but my boyfriend — I know, he's not a boy but I am not a girl either but we are friends," she laughed, tossing back her head and then continuing, "my boyfriend, his name is Harold. Well, he comes with me. We plan to take it easy sometimes, go out for dinner, rest a little bit, maybe get a motel room, and head back to our apartment in Northridge in the morning. We never know exactly what we are going to do. It depends on how we feel. I hope you understand? I mean it would be great to carpool and all, but that's one of the things about being retired, we can do what we want, take a little time to rest and so on and so forth. But Harold keeps telling me not to get too used to it because when I win the pageant we are going to be busy every single weekend running all over the Tri-Rivers."

She flashed a great smile and tossed her head in a raucous laugh. "Hey, I need to hurry and get into my costume. They'll be checking us out, you know, making sure we are all presentable. I'm singing "New York, New York," and did I mention I'm from New York?" She winked and threw back her head and laughed again. "I'm glad you understand, sweetheart. I have to hurry now. Harold can't wait to see me do my thing."

She started to rush off to change into her costume but suddenly turned around, walked back a few steps and looked at Kate as if she had just noticed something. "Hey, nice hair!" she said with her big laugh, and gave her a thumbs up.

Kate smiled. She hadn't said one word the whole time. She tried to imagine what it would be like to share a ride from Northridge with Myrna and Harold and was perfectly happy to know they had other plans.

The dressing room teemed with activity. Stephanie tugged at her hot pink tights, Carol was awash in feathers and beads, and Rosemarie was an unusual vision in a shredded skirt and tattered flowers. On the far side of the room, Sherry struggled with her costume, a pale peach taffeta dress, off the shoulders, cinched at the waist and ballooning out over a hoop skirt. She looked frantic, and Kate hurried over to see if she could help. "Oh yes, please!" Sherry said, "I hoped the Happy Hookers could help me but they are so busy with everyone else."

Kate buttoned and hooked her into the dress. "Beautiful, just beautiful, Sherry," she said. Sherry did not respond. She was adjusting her hair around her ears.

Suddenly it was time. "Hello ladies!" called Harriet, standing at the entry to the dressing room. "Before we begin the talent rehearsal, let me review. I will call your name in performance order. Please walk to the center of the stage, smile, and stand there for us to see you. Then turn around so we can see the back of your costume. Go slowly. We need to see all of your costume, every detail. If there is a problem, now is the time to find out about it. We may ask to have a few words with you somewhat privately. We don't have to shout it out for everyone to hear. And of course we will let you know if your costume is approved.

"When we have finished evaluating your costume, we will ask you to go to the spot where you will begin your talent performance. Some of you will be off stage, some will be on. Go there and wait for your cue to begin. The sound technicians are standing by with your music and microphones and special lighting as appropriate.

"We want all of you to enjoy watching every one of the performances if you wish. I think this will give you a greater appreciation for our show. You can take a seat in the auditorium to watch, or if you prefer you can remain back stage until the final act ends. Either way is fine. Finally, when the rehearsal is over please be seated in the auditorium. We will have some final announcements before you return to the dressing room. Any questions?

"All right then, please get ready to come on stage when I call your name." The whirlwind of color and activity swept toward the door, down the hall and onto the side stage.

Harriet seated herself at a table off to the side

of the stage area. Shuffling through a few papers, she located the performance order and reviewed it briefly.

"Anita Archer. Come on out and let us see your costume for your piano solo, "Piano Roll Blues." Anita was all smiles as she walked onto the stage. Her costume was a white dinner jacket with a row of black sequins around the collar and lapels. Under the jacket she wore a silver blouse and a black ribbon tie at the neck.

"Here's my hat," she announced, setting a black top hat jauntily on her head, "I got it at Save-A-Lot for just 99 cents!" Wearing black slacks and her silver shoes, she turned around to complete the modeling of her costume.

"A word with you please," said Harriet, motioning her to come close to the table where they sat at the side of the stage. "Your costume is approved. One thing, Anita. We have been over this before. Please do not walk around backstage nor down the hall to and from the dressing room without your shoes. No bare feet. Understood?"

Anita nodded. "I promise, except when I am playing the piano. I can't play with those shoes on but I get the idea. Thanks."

The piano was near the back of the stage. "Not so far back," Harriet Anderson told the stagehands. "She needs to be closer to the audience." They pushed it forward and then pushed it sideways. "There. Perfect." They sauntered off stage.

Anita certainly didn't hold back, and in spite of the silver shoes she hustled across the stage to the piano. Sliding onto the bench, she caressed the side of the upright piano and ran her fingers up and down the keyboard.

"Bar room music, that's what I like to play," Anita had explained earlier. It was her favorite style, big enough to be heard by everyone in a bar and with a big beat that everyone wanted to move to. "Piano Roll Blues," the song she had chosen, featured a mighty big beat which she pounded out not only with her foot but with her whole leg. She kicked off the objectionable silver shoes and planted her right foot on the pedal, her left foot arched on the floor beside her, and let the rhythm roll.

The audience was delighted and most people hummed and sang along. It was that kind of song. Hadn't Liberace played it back in the day? Hadn't he grinned at the TV camera as he flourished and posed through the song? Anita frolicked across the keys and created that same magic. Everyone in the audience kept time, bouncing along with the music. The whole thing took just under the two-minutes-and-thirty-second limit, plenty of time to spare when Anita ran her fingers down the keyboard with a great flourish. She felt for her shoes with her toes, slipped them on, pushed back the bench and stood to take a bow.

"Way to go, Anita!" shouted her husband from somewhere in the middle of the auditorium.

"Thanks Mr. Nick!" she called back to him, and gave him a tip of her fancy black hat.

"Stephanie McCoy," announced Harriet Anderson. "Come on out and show us your costume for your modern dance to "Pink Panther." Stephanie crossed the stage wearing a skin tight hot pink leotard, all one piece, and she did not look comfortable. A black belt, obviously too tight, squeezed her waist. Her plain brown hair was pulled back under a black headband adorned with black kitty ears. She straightened it as she walked on stage, but it slipped backwards on her head and she straightened it again.

After she modeled the costume Harriet said, "A word with you, Stephanie." With her voice lowered, she said to Stephanie, "As I said earlier, one of the things we try to encourage is a smooth and, shall we say, a bulge-free look. In your pink leotard, we notice some bulging."

Stephanie made a face and laughed, "You noticed 'some' bulging? Some? Why do you think I am so uncomfortable?"

Harriet laughed with her. "Perhaps you can find something to wear underneath? I think that will help. And one more thing, make sure your headband is secure. Pin it in place or add an elastic band. We don't want it flying off while you dance. Wear your costume next week so we can approve it."

Holding on to her headband with cat ears, she nodded to the sound technician and struck a pose. The music began. Her performance consisted of striking one pose, then another pose of the Pink Panther and tip-toeing between poses.

"Judith Ann Cole. Please show us your costume for your performance. How lovely that you composed this song yourself." With the help of her walking cane, Judith made her way across the stage. She wore a long black choir robe with a square white collar and a scarlet red satin bow at the neck. Under it she wore a plain knit black dress, and the sleeves peeked out from the wide and loose sleeves of the robe.

"I borrowed this robe from my church choir," she explained. "My performance does not require any props or anything else. I sing *a cappella*, without any accompaniment. I prefer to use a regular standing microphone, please."

"Judith Ann," said Harriet Anderson, "you look very nice, but we just don't want you to get overheated. These stage lights can be rather warm and you are actually wearing two dresses. Please find a lightweight dress or perhaps a slip or some other simple, cool garment to wear under the choir robe. We don't want to see you pass out from the heat of the stage lights." It was the first time anyone had mentioned the heat of the stage lights.

Judith Ann was already unzipping the robe, warm from wearing it over the dress. "Good idea," she said, fanning herself with her hand then lifting her hair off the back of her neck.

Harriet nodded, "Just let us see it next week and give our approval."

Standing at the stage microphone, Judith Ann sang "I Saw the Way" completely *a cappella*, no piano, no guitar, just her own voice, unaccompanied.

Her voice was not quite soprano, nor was it quite alto. She sang in both ranges. She had a little trouble reaching the high notes but assured Harriet she would work on this. Harriet Anderson asked her how she would define her voice. "Mezzo soprano," Judith Ann answered, "meaning I can sing both alto and soprano."

Harriet Anderson paused to make a note about this. She had explained to the ladies that sometimes she noted tidbits of information which might be useful for the MC when introducing the candidates during the pageant. This was in addition to the biographical information each candidate had submitted as part of their application. "Knowing your voice is a mezzo soprano will be very interesting to our audience, Judith Ann. Thank you, it was lovely."

"Olga Asamova, we are ready for you. Show us your costume for your clogging routine to "Mountain Music." Olga bounced energetically onto the stage wearing denim jeans rolled up over her calf, a jeweled belt, a red plaid shirt, and a sporty red felt cowgirl hat. Her clogging shoes looked similar to cowboy boots, but had thick soles and wide buckles.

Harriet did not hesitate. "Your costume looks great, Olga. Approved. I can't wait to see your new clogging routine. Please begin."

"Clogging," Olga had explained that morning as everyone dressed for rehearsal, "is a folk dance in which the dancer strikes the heel, the toe, or both against the floor or each other to create musical rhythms. To make it easier to understand, sometimes it has been referred to as flatfooting, foot-stomping, buck dancing, clog dancing, jigging and other local terms."

The ubiquitous Eleanor Butler had stopped by the dressing room before making her way to the auditorium. She stood by with her cane in hand, listening to the long explanation. When Olga finished, Eleanor Butler snapped, "Who cares? We just want to see you dance. We saw you last year. Let's see what you have for us this year."

Kate and the others watched Eleanor leave the dressing room. "She certainly says what she has on her mind," said Olga, smiling. Kate remembered the word she had chosen to describe Olga: Confident. The comments of Eleanor Butler did not seem to faze her in the least, in fact, she was amused.

Olga cued the sound technician to start the music she hoped would be familiar to many: "Mountain Music." Dressed in denim and red, she clogged across the stage with a huge smile on her face.

Most people in the audience knew the song and quickly started to clap along with her and stamp their feet to the rhythm. Someone in the audience whooped, "Yee haw!"

Olga smiled, looped her thumbs in her jeweled belt, and took a bow. She was still clogging when she disappeared behind the curtain.

"Angeline Zolta," called Harriet Anderson. "We are ready to see your costume for your performance. I believe you are singing "Unforgettable."

Slowly and purposefully, Angeline walked across the stage, stopped, then turned so that Harriet and the others could see her costume front and back. She wore a simple sleeveless white silk dress with a V-neck, no pleats or ruffles. The white silk was a stunning contrast to her black skin. For accessories she wore a wide gold bracelet, a gold neck cuff and gold hoop earrings, her jet black hair pulled back tight to accentuate the jewelry.

"Angeline, your outfit is truly elegant. Your

costume is approved. Do you plan to use the standing microphone for your performance, or would you prefer a lavalier microphone?"

"I prefer the lavalier so I can move about a little while I sing," said Angeline. "I'll just clip it here," she added, gesturing to the seam at her neckline.

"Fine," said Harriet, making a note of it. "We will notify the sound crew to have one ready for you."

No matter what she did, Angeline had a look of serene elegance about her. Kate thought of the descriptive words she had chosen for her: Strong and Elegant. They suited her perfectly. When she gave her philosophy, she did it in measured and graceful tones. Her selection of the famous Nat King Cole song, "Unforgettable," suited her perfectly too. Smooth and polished, Kate thought.

"Carol Parcellia," announced Harriet after Angeline left the stage. "Please show us your costume for your Tahitian dance. I have no idea how to pronounce the title." She attempted to say the words phonetically. "*Ua Tai Au Ia Oe-Aparima*, is that correct?"

Carol laughed and repeated the title, emphasizing how to say it properly. She was barefoot, resplendent in a combination of a tall green and yellow feather headdress, multi-colored flowered top and billowing green grass skirt. She held decorated gourds in each hand.

"These," she explained holding the gourds, "are for shaking in rhythm to the music when I dance. And I assure you, the skirt and top are quite secure for the dance and all the hip and body shaking it requires."

Harriet Anderson smiled, asking "Can you give us a little example?" Carol turned and shook her hips. "Wonderful! Your costume is approved with one very important reminder," said Harriet Anderson. "You must wear shoes before and after your performance, on the side stage and in the hallways. No bare feet."

Carol moved to the side stage to make her entry from there. She held the decorated gourds in each hand and shimmied her hips as vigorously as she shook the gourds, keeping up with the wild rhythm of the drums and song.

Someone in the audience whistled loudly, a wolf whistle as they used to be called. Was that her husband? "Hey, get back to work!" she called to him over her shoulder, and shimmied her hips all the way to the side of the stage as she exited.

Everyone laughed at Carol's sassy exit, even Harriet Anderson. "That was a good performance, Carol," she said, "and your exit reminds me of something I want to ask everyone else to do."

Now everyone got quiet, even Carol's husband who had laughed with delight at Carol's playful departure. Kate and the others waited to hear what Harriet had to say.

"It is a good idea to think of yourself as a character when you perform, no matter what you are doing. Whether you are dancing, singing, or giving a monologue, think of yourself as a character as you enter the stage, while you are on stage, and as you leave the stage. Do what Carol just did, stay in character as you exit." She paused and looked at Carol's husband, seated just a few rows back, then she continued. "I don't recommend shouting at your husband," she said with a very big smile, "but you get the idea."

Teresa Rodriguez waited the few seconds while everyone chatted about Harriet's instruction. At last Harriet announced, "Come on out, please, Teresa. Show us your costume. Your bio says you are a Western singer but I believe I know this lovely song. Is it from *The Fantasticks*? Did we make an error? Is this a Western song?"

Teresa smiled, carrying her guitar with a wide strap over her shoulder. "No, you did not make an error. "They Were You" is such a beautiful song it can be sung in almost any genre. When my husband and I had a little trio, we sang all kinds of songs. Sometimes we sang Broadway songs as Western, and sometimes we sang Western as Broadway. I will sing "They Were You" accompanied by typical Western guitar chords. You will see it fits the Western style very well."

Teresa wore a royal blue western shirt and a blue scarf tied at the neck. The yoke of the shirt dripped with gold fringe that swayed every time she swayed. Her pants were gold tights styled like jeans, with tiny fake back pockets. Completing her outfit were white high heeled cowboy boots with gold tipped toes and a large white cowboy hat, which she carried in her free hand. Her curly dark hair was pinned back.

Harriet waved a little gesture for her to come over. "Teresa, your outfit is approved. I have some concerns about your guitar. I must ask you to keep it in its case backstage. There will be a lot of activity the night of the show. Please do not leave your guitar out where it might be in the way or get damaged or cause someone to fall."

Teresa nodded, "Of course. Just so you know, it is my habit to actually wear my guitar whenever it is out of the case. That is I why I have this strap. I wear it over my shoulder. I would like to use a lavalier microphone please, but it will not affect how I wear the guitar."

Teresa walked to the side of the stage. Earlier, she had told Kate she preferred to wait to begin her song. She wanted to be in the center of the stage and look directly at the audience. "No singing while I'm walking in," she said, "it's more personal this way."

Earlier she had also wondered aloud, "Should I put on the hat before I go on stage, or after?" Now, as she stood at the side of the stage, she firmly put the hat on her head and closed her eyes, concentrating.

"Okay!" she said to no one in particular, although her voice was picked up by the microphone. She strutted out onto the stage, smiling at the audience who had heard her say "Okay" and was delighted to see her. The gold fringe on the royal blue shirt swayed as she strummed and sang "They Were You."

It had been years since Kate had heard the song, and she leaned forward to hear every word. Halfway through the song, Kate took a quick glance around and wondered how many in the audience would try to remember when or where they had heard this fantastic song before. She could tell there were many who remembered as they sang along quietly with Teresa.

Tears filled Teresa's eyes when she sang the final stanza. She added a few words at the end, softly spoken in Spanish, *esta es, esta es, es usted.*

The audience was hushed when Harriet Anderson gently said to her, "No crying, dear. No crying."

Teresa took a seat in the audience, next to Kate. She placed her hat in her lap and breathed deeply.

While she waited for the next performance, she leaned over and whispered, "That song makes me think of my husband. Of course that's why I chose it. We sang that together in our little trio, but the words, the words, they are so special." she said. "I miss him so much. I sure hope I don't cry when I sing it the night of the pageant."

Kate looked around again. More than one old Queen was putting away the tissue she'd used to dab her eyes. "Well if you do, there might be some others crying with you," Kate responded.

"Bonnie Gabriel," called Harriet Anderson. "Please show us your costume for your comedy act which you call 'Mildred'." Bonnie wore a loose house dress, an unbuttoned pink cardigan sweater, big black sunglasses, and little knit hat. Her white socks were rolled down to her blue tennis shoes. Harriet Anderson couldn't help but laugh, "You look just like the character, Maxine."

Bonnie stopped and stared at her with a particularly sour expression. "Maxine? The one on the greeting cards? The one in the funny papers? Are you trying to be funny?" she quipped. "Please don't try to confuse me!" Harriet laughed again. Bonnie Gabriel's comedy routine was a welcome change from the emotion of Teresa's performance.

Bonnie went on, "And don't try to trick me with some sort of fancy microphone all hidden in my

sweater or something. Just a regular standing microphone, if it's not too much trouble."

"Yes, of course, a regular mic, please" she told
the sound technicians. "Bonnie, your costume is
approved. Please proceed with your performance."

"Hi, I'm Mildred, maybe some of you know me?
A lot of people say I remind them of Maxine. Do
any of you know her? " People nodded and laughed.
"Well get over it," she snapped. "I'm Mildred."

"I'm a single senior citizen but I decided what
the heck, it might be fun to go out on a date. It's
never too late. So I found a web site called 'Single
Seniors Gone Wild.' You guessed it, they were wild
bird watchers.

"I may be a senior but I have the same needs
as any other red blooded woman: candy, donuts,
cookies, ice cream." The audience loved it.

"Is anyone here looking for a man? Come on,
admit it. Okay honey, here are some tips," and she
gave advice about things to watch for such as what
he might claim to be a recent photo. "If it looks
exactly like a 1950's yearbook picture, it probably
is. Or if the guy seems to be wearing a Halloween
costume, take a real careful look and make sure it IS
a Halloween costume, if you know what I mean."

True to her character, Bonnie put her hands on
her hips and scowled at the audience even though she
received a big round of applause when she finished.

Harried Anderson called for Helen Nicholas. "May we see your costume for your performance of "Sunrise, Sunset"? I believe it is from *Fiddler on the Roof*, and it is such a lovely song."

Helen walked onto the stage wearing a long dress of shimmering bronze satin, with elbow length sleeves and a flared skirt. Her hair was held back with a wide tortoise shell headband, revealing her serene face. She carried a single lighted candle which flickered just enough to light up her face. Walking slowly to the center of the stage, she focused straight ahead, beyond the candle.

Alarmed, Harriet rose to her feet. "Helen, I must ask you to put out that candle immediately, it is a fire hazard!" she demanded.

Helen stopped. She turned the candle upside down and shook it. "It's not real. It's a flashlight with some little pieces of fabric that look like a flame." she explained, smiling. "We use them in our Christmas pageant when we sing Handel's *Messiah*." She switched the candle-flashlight off and on to demonstrate.

"Amazing, it looks so real," said Harriet, taking her seat. "Of course you can use the candle; it is quite dramatic, and I definitely approve it. And the rest of your costume is also approved. Which kind of microphone would you prefer?"

Helen preferred the lavalier microphone. "I'll

clip in on and forget about it, and that way I can keep my focus," she said.

Helen Nicholas kept pretty much to herself most of the time, but each time Kate looked at her she was touched by her natural beauty. That was the word she'd chosen for her. Beautiful. Kate watched her enter from stage left as the music began and thought she must have been stunning in her youth because here in the Ms. Senior Tri-Rivers Pageant her face, her beautiful sad face, could still launch a thousand ships.

Helen sang "Sunrise, Sunset" softly at first, the candle in her hand. The audience was very quiet, enchanted by her every word. As she sang, Kate stood up and quietly moved out of the row of seats, left the auditorium by the side exit, and went down the hall to the stage entrance. She was the next person in the performance order; it was time for her to get in place. She could still hear Helen singing. The auditorium was quiet, almost like a church as Kate tiptoed onto the side stage. And when she peeked through the curtains to look at the audience, she saw several people dabbing their eyes. Teresa wasn't the only one whose performance brought tears. Helen had showered the audience with her love, her pain as well.

"Kate Dearborn," Harriet said, looking over the performance list. The audience was still hushed from Helen's performance.

"Please show us your costume for your recitation of two poems by Robert Frost. Which poems are they?"

Kate answered, "The Road Not Taken" and "Stopping by Woods on a Snowy Evening." She added, "I prefer to use just a regular standing stage microphone, please."

Harriet Anderson nodded and seemed to be familiar with both poems. "And about your costume, Kate, may I have a word with you?" Kate walked over to the table, her plain black shoes tapping on the quiet stage floor. Her simple gray dress hardly moved, unlike some other costumes that swayed and ruffled with every step.

"Kate, I have something for you from Eleanor Butler, one of the former Queens."

Harriet did not need to explain. Kate knew exactly who Eleanor was but she did not know why the old Queen would have something for her. "What?" she asked. "I don't understand."

Harriet handed her a small shopping bag with the name Windsor's Fine Apparel printed on it. Kate had no idea who or what Windsor's was but reached inside the bag.

Harriet went on, "Eleanor saw your costume a little earlier this morning and thought this might make it a bit more special. Like all good Queens, she had it in her car." The white tissue paper rustled as Kate pulled out and unwrapped the item. It was the gray silk shawl with the long beaded fringe that Eleanor Butler had worn that first day at the kick-off meeting. "She offers it to you, but of course the decision is yours. She asked me to tell you it will add a little bling to your costume. I think she means all those silver beads in the fringe. She also says it will look nice with your new hairdo."

"My hairdo?" Surprised, Kate reached up and tousled her hair just slightly.

"Yes, I've been meaning to mention it too. Very nice, dear."

"Thank you! And about the shawl, I love it. Please tell Eleanor thank you. I will as well, of course, when I see her." Kate put the shawl over her shoulders and let it slip down around her arms. It felt like a caress. "It's lovely," she said, and felt tears start to well in her eyes. Oh no. More tears, she thought. Blinking to hold them back, she turned to model the dress and the shawl for Harriet Anderson. Her costume was approved.

Now it was Kate's turn to walk on stage for her talent performance. To her, it seemed like a long walk to the standing microphone, and she was still uncomfortable looking out at the audience. Taking a deep breath, she introduced the two poems: "The Road Not Taken" by Robert Frost, followed by "Stopping by Woods on a Snowy Evening" by Robert Frost.

Kate had chosen the two poems because they so perfectly expressed her own feelings about decisions and choices she made in her own life, how there are times in our lives – her life – where we must choose between two options, and decide which way to go. The choice makes all the difference in what lies ahead. And sometimes we have promises to keep and cannot venture into lovely woods, no matter how dark and deep and enticing they are. We must stay the course we are on.

Kate recited both poems from memory, without the aid of notes. She found herself stammering at times, but at least she had the poems memorized. She held back the sigh of relief inside her when she finished. Well aware of her stammers and falters, she was not surprised to find she had run over the two-and-a-half minute time limit.

"Keep working on it Kate, and cut about twenty seconds off," said Harriet Anderson. Kate assured her she would. She continued to be amazed at how hard it was to do this.

Taking a seat beside Teresa, she whispered, "I wish I could be invisible in my plain gray dress and plain black shoes and just tiptoe out of here right about now."

Teresa covered her mouth to suppress a giggle. "I wouldn't worry about it, but I suppose you could hide under your pretty new shawl," she whispered back.

"Jane Morrison, we are ready to see your costume for your dance interpretation of "The Way You Make Me Feel." This is a Michael Jackson song, I believe. What an entertainer he was!" Jane walked out onto the stage not only in costume, but in character. She had mastered the moonwalk.

Her costume was a bright red jacket, white shirt, and black pants with rolled up cuffs. She wore white sox with black shoes and clutched a black hat just a few inches above her head. Her free hand glittered in a knit silver glove. She spun around to show the back of the costume.

"A word with you, Jane," said Harriet Anderson. "No hologram of Michael, please. One Michael is quite enough," she said with a wink. Not everyone would know she was referring to the hologram performance of Michael Jackson which was shown in Las Vegas at a Billboard Awards ceremony, but Jane knew what she meant and tipped her hat. "Your costume is approved," said Harriet Anderson.

Jane whirled and posed, slid sideways and backwards, pranced and gyrated. "Heck, I don't have any choreography," she had laughed before the performance, "I just do what the music tells me until it shuts off in two-and-a-half minutes." When Jane exited the stage backwards, she was still doing the moonwalk.

"That's what I mean about staying in character," said Harriet Anderson. She joined the audience in their applause as Jane kicked her black shoes with the white sox one more time.

"Myrna Brenner, please show us your costume for your performance of 'New York, New York.'" When Harriet Anderson looked up, she could not contain the look of surprise that came over her face. Myrna wore a very short frothy net and lace dress, its double layer net skirt flaring wide just above her knees. The low cut strapless top zipped up the middle. A wide elastic belt cinched her waist. The color was a peculiar gray green color called Seafoam. It was not the dress alone that surprised Harriet; it was also the very large spiked crown, made of Styrofoam, sprayed green, and the large Styrofoam torch in her hand.

Strutting across the stage in the tall black patent leather platform boots that reached above her knees, she shouted, "New York, baby, New York!" as she thrust the torch over her head.

Harriet seemed to need a moment to gain her composure. "Yes," she said, making a note on the paper in front of her, "and it's a hell of a town if I recall."

Myrna threw back her head and laughed, "You're all right, Harriet Anderson."

After a quick consultation with her two

assistants, Harriet smiled and said, "A word with you please, Myrna."

"Coming," she said, staying in character and strutting across the stage holding the torch high.

"What an exciting idea, to be the Statue of Liberty, Lady Liberty," said Harriet. "But we have one small concern about your costume. The green bra shows above the dress, and viewing a bra and its straps under your strapless dress, well, it is distracting."

Myrna bit her lip, then explained, "Well I didn't think you would want me to go braless, I mean I listened to all you said about being modest and appropriate and all. So I thought wearing a bra under the dress was a good idea. And it's green and all," she added defensively.

Harriet Anderson quickly responded, "How very clever of you," and Myrna relaxed a little. Harriet continued, "I have an offer – strictly up to you, of course. Earlier, another former Queen offered something to Kate, it happened to be a lovely shawl. She offered it, but it was strictly up to Kate to decide if she wanted to use it. Kate accepted."

Myrna stepped closer to listen. "As you know, we Queens carry all sorts of costumes in our cars, and other things we might need for appearances. I happen to have a beautiful undergarment in my car, a Merry Widow, which I would be happy to lend to you to use instead of the green bra with the exposed straps. It's black lace, but I don't think it will show so it doesn't make any difference. I can bring it in, and you can try it on, see what you think. Perhaps Lady Liberty will be even more attractive without the green bra and straps showing, but of course it is totally up to you." Delighted, Myrna said she would love to try it on.

Following the costume consultation, Myrna returned to the side of the stage, a bundle of energy waiting to do her thing. The technician started the musical accompaniment to "New York, New York" right on cue but in her excitement, Myrna missed it, chiming in with the lyrics way too late. And off key. It took her six measures to figure it out. "Stop, stop, stop!" she ordered, stomping and gesturing to the sound tech. "I couldn't even hear that. Louder, much louder! I need loud music for this song!" The tech started it again.

Sensing trouble for Myrna, her boyfriend Harold grabbed his NY Yankees hat and hustled down from the rear of the auditorium to get closer to the stage. He took an aisle seat and tried to catch her attention as she began to sing the song made famous by Frank Sinatra and Lisa Minnelli.

"Atta girl, Babe! Sing it!" he called to her, clapping loudly. Myrna flashed her great smile at him and visibly relaxed.

Angeline sat in the row behind Harold and without any hesitation began clapping her hands in time with the music, calling "Come on Myrna, sing it!"

Then Anita joined in saying, "Mmmm hmmm, sing it girl," and pretty soon everyone was moving to the rhythm of the song, and no one cared how badly off key she was.

As she headed to the final lyrics, she may have been off key and very loud, but she finished up in fine style, holding her torch high above the spiky crown while everyone applauded.

Hurrying off the stage to take her seat near Harold, Myrna could not contain her excitement. "Harriet loves my song!" she exclaimed, still holding the torch, her hands flying and punctuating the air. "She just wants me to get in a couple of other practices, you know, so those sound techs can get the cue and the level right, you know, so they won't mess me up. And she has this Merry Widow thing for me to wear, she thinks it might be just right for under the strapless dress. Hey, and she's the boss. Maybe I can get the girls to help me fasten it up in the dressing room."

Kate smiled as she watched Harold slip his arm around Myrna and whisper, "You were great, Babe, and your costume too." He gently removed her Miss Liberty crown and put it in his lap. His arm still around her, he said ever so softly, even tenderly, "Shhhhhhh, Babe, here's Sandi." Myrna kissed his cheek and put her torch in the seat next to them.

"Sandi Meredith, we are ready to see your costume for 'Dinner Table Magic.' And I understand you also have some props for your performance. Please bring them out too."

The stage hands carried a card table to the center of the stage and draped a black tablecloth over it. Sandi Meredith stood in the wings and waited until they added a place mat and a set of silverware: knife, fork, and two large soup spoons. She wore a white shirt and black pants and waved a big red napkin, which she tucked into the neck of her shirt when she got to the table. "A lavalier microphone for me, please," she requested.

"I can hardly wait for your magic," said Harriet Anderson. "And I have a question about your costume. We want to be sure the knife is, well, not a weapon. Do we sound like the TSA? It is a plain dinner knife, isn't it?" When Sandi assured her that it was harmless, her costume was approved.

"Hey everybody," she waved to the audience. "I'm Sandi Meredith, number 13. Do you feel lucky? Do you? Well tonight is your lucky night. We are going to have a little dinner table magic. Have you ever been at a dinner table and things are really boring? We are about to change that." She bowed, then sat down in the chair. Smiling, she pointed to the knife on the table. "How about making the knife just disappear? Maybe you could swallow it."

Swallow it? Now she had the attention of the audience. Sure enough, with a quick sweep of her hand and a gurgle and a slurp, the knife disappeared. The audience applauded.

"Or, you can always make things better by adding a little sugar. Not artificial sweetener, real sugar! She held up a pink packet of sugar substitute in one hand, rubbed it between her palms and suddenly, when she opened the other hand, the pink packet was gone and there was a brown packet of plain, real sugar in its place. More applause.

"Or if things get really boring, you can always play the spoons!" She picked up the two soup spoons and holding them just so in one hand, she bounced them together in a lively rhythm. Everyone applauded and she stood up to take a bow. Unfortunately, the "disappearing knife" which had disappeared into her lap during her sleight of hand, dropped from her lap when she stood up. "Oops! I will work on that," she assured Harriet Anderson.

"Sherry Springfield?" Harriet looked around for her. "May we see your costume for your performance of 'Shall We Dance?' Wait a moment, we have two songs listed here. The other is 'I Could Have Danced All Night.'" Sherry emerged from the side stage in her peach taffeta gown, the skirt billowing wide over the hoops. "Sherry, can you tell us which song you are performing, please?" Sherry did not respond, so Harriet repeated, "Can you tell us which song?"

Sherry looked around the stage as if she was unsure of where to go. "Here," whispered a stage hand as he walked out and took her by the hand. "Stand right over here."

Suddenly realizing that Harriet and her assistants were seated to the side of the stage, Sherry turned to them. "I'm sorry, what did you say?" Harriet Anderson repeated the question. Sherry answered, "My song is "Shall We Dance?" from *The King and I*. It's just that in the beginning I could not choose my favorite, I have loved them both so much over the years." Sherry assured Harriet there would be no further confusion and apologized for her distraction just then. "It will be fine, I promise you."

"Very well," said Harriet, making a note.

Sherry continued, "And please, may I have a lavalier microphone to wear? I actually plan to dance just a little during my performance. Won't these hoop skirts look lovely as I swirl around?" She picked them up lightly in front to demonstrate.

Harriet Anderson nodded, "Yes they will be lovely but you must be very careful." She approved Sherry's costume. "May we see your performance now?"

Seated next to Kate, Teresa leaned over and whispered, "I love that song. I heard it so often when I was growing up. I remember Yul Brynner in *The King and I*. That's where I learned the lyrics. I loved to watch him, his arms folded while he sang with Deborah Kerr, remember? And he made me swoon when he danced with her. I wish I could dance like that."

Kate agreed, "It's one of those songs everyone loves, no one ever gets tired of it. Even I can sing along. As for me dancing, forget it."

Teresa leaned closer and whispered even lower. "Sometimes this seems so difficult for Sherry, though. Not her singing, that's lovely. I mean she gets confused, doesn't seem to hear some of the things going on. I hope you don't think I am gossiping, I am just concerned. Am I the only one who sees this?"

Kate whispered her reply, "No, I have noticed it too. I hate to see her having a hard time, don't you?"

With her delicate beauty, Sherry was becoming a favorite among many in the audience. A few seats away, Bonnie commented in whisper loud enough to be heard by several others around her, "I was never as delicate as Sherry Springfield, even when I was a baby. She is like a flower."

Amazed, Kate whispered to Teresa, "That's what I always think of too. She reminds me of roses."

The audience hushed as Sherry made her way to

the center of the stage, entering from the left, looking around as if she was entering a ball, gently holding her taffeta skirt over the hoops.

With a nod of her head to cue the music, Sherry began to sing, her lovely voice lilting through the verses of "Shall We Dance?" Halfway through, she daintily took the skirt and hoops in her hands and danced in small loops as she sang the chorus. It was beautiful, lyrical, romantic, and the audience loved it. The timing was perfect and the song ended at precisely two-and-a-half minutes.

"Thank you," Sherry said breathlessly, almost as an exhale. Everyone applauded loudly. Sherry lifted her hoops and skirt and stayed in character, all the way off the stage. Such a lovely woman, Kate thought. Still, she wondered what it was that made her seem so fragile.

Harriet tapped on the microphone, reminding the audience that there were others waiting to rehearse. "Rosemarie North. Please show us your costume for your soliloquy as Ophelia. This is from *Hamlet*, isn't it? And please show us any props you might require."

Rosemarie staggered onto the stage in full character, immersed in the role of Ophelia. Her pale blue dress was shredded to mere tatters. Beneath the dress she wore long white tights, on her feet were black ballet slippers. "This is exactly how my costume should be, all shredded and torn," she stated, dropping out of character to address Harriet Anderson. Her thick white hair was rumpled and messy, falling forward into her eyes. "Ophelia was crazy with madness, you know, and would not have bothered to comb her hair," Rosemarie continued. "I was thinking of wearing a wig, but everything looked too fake!" She wore a few tattered silk flowers stuck in her hair. For her stage prop she had just one chair. She would begin the scene walking in a circle around the chair.

"I see," said Harriet Anderson. "And because you will be walking around the chair, may we assume that you prefer a lavalier mic?" Rosemarie nodded and Harriet made a note.

"Rosemarie, you must use great care in your madness. No accidents. We can't have you fall to the floor and hurt yourself. Please shorten the shreds of your skirt to no more than ankle length to avoid any possibility of tripping on them. Pull your hair back and out of your eyes and be sure that no flowers fall into your eyes, please. You need to be able to see. We must ask you to wear your costume again next week, with the adjustments, so we can approve it then."

Rosemarie threw her arms out and declared, "Of course! I don't want to trip and fall either!" She could not seem to resist the opportunity to be dramatic on the stage. "I am ready now," she added solemnly.

She began the scene with one hand on the back of the chair, then slowly circled as her voice rang out in a mixture of giddy and somber tones. Oh my, how she carried on as the mad and mournful Ophelia.

Breathing hard, she leaned on the chair during the latter part of her soliloquy, grabbing the seat to help lower herself to the floor. Her knees clearly hurt as she made a final landing. At last she fell backwards gasping Ophelia's final words, "Good night, good night."

There was complete silence as she lay on the floor. Suddenly she raised her head and waved vigorously. "Harriet! Oh Harriet," she called loudly. "The lights are supposed to go down before I stand up and get off the stage."

Harriet prompted the technician to watch carefully for the end of Rosemarie's scene so she could get off the stage. The lights went off as a stage hand hurried over to help her get up. A delighted audience applauded at Rosemarie's entertainment.

When the lights came up again, Harriet called for Marcia Van Horne. "Please show us your costume for your jazz dance performance." Last on the list of performers, Marcia had waited by herself at the rear of the stage. Typical of Marcia, she had not joined the others in line at the side of the stage nor in the audience and only now emerged from the darkness. Stepping onto the stage she smiled brilliantly and stretched her long legs in a sideward slide to make her entry, then tipped her red satin top hat trimmed with black. She dazzled in a red satin body suit, black fishnet stockings with perfect seams up the back of each leg, and red stiletto heels. Red hot, thought Kate.

With a big smile, Harriet Anderson announced, "Congratulations, Marcia. Your costume is gorgeous and it is approved."

Harriet signaled the light technician to dim the stage lights as Marcia took center stage. When the lights came up in a single spot light, Marcia stood with her hands on her hips, smiling at the audience. She waited for the music to begin. Word had spread that her dance teacher, Lyle Johnston, was in the audience to see her rehearse. Johnston had danced in several big musicals in New York and as a backup dancer for various celebrities. Several years ago he returned to his home town in the Tri-Rivers region and ran a successful dancing school in upscale Devonville. The buzz was that Marcia was his prize student. She'd been in one of his shows as a soloist and had bedazzled the audience. It was a fair assumption that she would do the same with "All That Jazz."

Marcia danced her way through the song with perfection. At exactly two minutes and twenty seconds she finished the dance with a grand finale, and ten seconds to spare. Everyone gasped when she slid one leg forward, hat in her hand held high above her head, and glided to the floor with her legs in a complete split. At age 63 she was as flexible as a child.

"Yowch," came several groans from the audience. Marcia still smiled brilliantly, never flinching. She got up and took a bow, long legs crossed in a graceful curtsy as everyone applauded.

With a tip of her hat to her dance teacher Lyle Johnston, she exited the stage in a long-legged strut, true to her red-hot character.

∿

The talent rehearsal was over. Once everyone was seated back in the auditorium, Harriet congratulated them for their performances and said there would be just a couple of reminders before today's rehearsal officially ended.

"First, as you all know, next week you must bring your gowns." Even though the schedule was well known, there was a murmur of excitement. "All gowns must be approved next week. Along with your gowns bring your undergarments, your shoes, your jewelry – everything you plan to wear in the gown competition. It's a big day, ladies, and we are getting closer and closer to the pageant. In less than a month, one of you will be crowned the new Queen, Ms. Senior Tri-Rivers."

"Second, plan your time and your transportation accordingly. Next Saturday is our luncheon, which will be right here in the Center immediately following our regular rehearsal. We expect it to end at about 1:30 pm. You, the candidates, will be our guests. Sorry, but no spouses, relatives, or friends this time, please. Eight of our former Queens are graciously preparing and hosting the lunch and it is just for you. You will be our guests.

"Third. Just a reminder that at the luncheon we will ask each of you to tell us a little more about yourself. Tell us something we might not know about you, because this is our "Getting to Know You" luncheon. Tell us why you entered the pageant. Don't worry and fret about it. No notes. No speeches. Just stand up and tell us about yourself in a relaxed and friendly setting.

"And this is the final announcement. Back during the kick-off meeting, I mentioned that some of our former Queens might have gowns to sell. Remember that? Well, a few of the Queens are here today, and they've brought along several of their gowns to sell. Good prices. Beautiful dresses. The gowns are hanging on dress racks out in the lobby. If anyone here still needs a gown, there might be something for you. Even if you don't need a gown, you might want to take a look anyway.

"And now you are all free to go, this rehearsal is over. See you next week!"

Myrna was the first to hurry out to the lobby. She held her jacket in one hand and a large canvas tote bag in the other. Placing them both in a chair in the lobby she turned to Harold, who was not far behind her. "Harold, watch these for me, please? There's a Merry Widow in that bag." He nodded and took a seat in one of the chairs, amused and entertained by all of the activity. Flipping quickly through dress after dress she pulled one off the rack and held it up to herself. "What do you think, Harold?" From his chair he nodded and smiled. Myrna walked closer to him. "It's a size 4, just my size. And for a redhead, emerald green is a really good color, don't you think?" Harold nodded again, smiling at Myrna's excitement.

The green crepe dress had yards of filmy green net that gathered in front at the waist, then went up over the bodice and fastened in back of the neck like a halter, then floated down the back all the way to the floor. The old Queen who owned the dress had stepped forward to talk with Myrna about it. "I need to tell you, the zipper is broken. Seems I am not a size 4 anymore. You will have to get it fixed."

Myrna looked it over. "Oh that's no big deal. I can pin it closed. Harold, what do you think?"

Harold nodded for a third time from his chair and declared, "It's beautiful Babe. You will be as beautiful as a mermaid or something with that thing floating down your back." Myrna waved the dress to make the back float like a mermaid. They laughed.

"Such a good price, too!" Myrna turned to the old Queen and announced, "I'll take it. Will you take cash? We don't have any credit!" She and Harold had a good laugh at that.

"Yes," answered the old Queen. "I hope it brings the best of luck to you."

Kate wasn't so lucky. There wasn't a dress in her size on the whole rack. She wondered if it was her imagination or did every old Queen really wear a size 2 or 4? Letting out a big sigh she accepted the reality that her search for a gown would continue and time was of the essence. There was just one week left to find that glamorous, long, sparkling, beautiful gown.

An Online Experience

The rain fell gently as Kate drove to one more shopping mall. After parking near the entry, she opened her umbrella and hoped for the best. Inside, she passed several stores but stopped to look in the window of the hip store Gotcha Girl, featuring skinny mannequins wearing formal dresses, fishnet stockings, and boots. She decided she might as well go inside to take a look. The music blared from the ceiling as Kate walked down the crowded aisle.

Languishing beside the counter was a clerk with silver studs in her pierced lips and blue tattoos on her arms and across her back. She wore one of those formal dresses the mannequins had on in the window. In her desperation Kate might have thought the neon green gown looked okay on the mannequin, and perhaps the black accessories and flashing lights had created some sort of illusion, but up close on the real body of the pierced and tattooed clerk it looked horrible.

"Excuse me," Kate said, backing away from the counter. "I think I am in the wrong store."

The clerk blinked, her black-rimmed eyes clearly bored with Kate. "No problem," she said. But it continued to be a big problem for Kate, and she headed for home.

"Lolita, it's stopped raining, let's go for a walk," Kate said to the happy little dog when she returned home. Lolita ran to the door. When they returned from the walk, the phone was ringing. Kate hurried to answer it. Delighted to hear her sister's voice, they talked about the adventures of being in a pageant. "The problem is, I can't find a gown," said Kate, "and time is getting short. I need a gown for the rehearsal next week."

"Kate, why don't you look online?" Colleen asked. "Megan tells me eBay has lots of dresses and Etsy has some really cool vintage clothes." Megan, Colleen's daughter, would know. To look at the way she dressed you could tell she knew a lot about clothes. She found fabulous coats, hats, pants and more at thrift stores, and recently she found some great knit tops on eBay and Etsy.

Kate was delighted. "Good idea, Colleen. I'll give it a try. Tell Megan thanks."

Key words: Gown. Dress. Pageant. Up popped some adorable baby dresses for little girls competing in toddler pageants.

Start again. *Key words:* Gown. Women's. Up popped some nightgowns.

Start again. *Key words:* Formal. Gown. Party. Up popped a lot of prom dresses. She was getting close.

Add more words: Pageant. Beads. *Add one final word:*

Black. I like black, thought Kate, and at least I won't get toddler dresses.

"And what to my wondering eyes should appear?" declared Kate, aloud. "One dress. MY dress!" She knew it was meant to be her dress the instant it popped up on the screen. "Vintage 1980s," read the description. "Used but good condition."

It was full-length with long mesh sleeves and a mesh cutout area between the jewel encrusted neck and the bodice. Heavy, elaborately beaded designs in gold, green and purple adorned the bodice, the neck, and the wrists. The entire dress was covered in black shiny beads. It was fabulous and she could hardly believe that amazingly, it was exactly her size, a 12.

Immediately, she began the process of purchasing it. She wanted to buy it before someone else did. Ignoring all the other payment choices, she clicked on Pay Now, entered her credit card information, and exhaled a big sigh. It was hers! Without any concern about cost, she selected the fastest shipping method possible: overnight. She wanted the dress tomorrow. It was exactly the dress she'd been dreaming of, looking for, hoping to find. She clicked back to look at the photos again, and smiled with even greater satisfaction each time she read the title: Mardi Gras Gown. The key words including black, party, and beads, had led her right to Mardi Gras. The heavy beadwork in green, purple and gold was definitely in the traditional Mardi Gras colors. Kate felt all the more excited when she imagined what fun it would be to wear it.

And it was fun! The first time she wore it for rehearsal Harriet Anderson took a long look at it and wrote something in her notes. Kate never knew what it was that Harriet wrote. She wondered, but didn't really care. It was her dress and she loved it.

Bonnie shrieked, "Look at Kate. She's got a Mardi Gras dress!" Shaking her hips, she said, "Hey girl, time to let the good times roll!"

Myrna promised to bring some beads. "Harold and I have some big, shiny Mardi Gras beads. You do know what the beads are for, don't you?" she winked.

Anita gave her a big hug, "Oh you are such a cute little Mardi Gras munchkin. Wait until Mr. Nick sees you. He has always wanted to go there."

Jane declared that the gown was a "Thriller" and Michael Jackson himself would approve.

Kate knew it wasn't a typical pageant gown. She hadn't been able to find a typical gown and in the end, found she didn't want one. All the fun and laughter about the Mardi Gras gown only made her love it more. While the other contestants looked fabulous in their red taffeta and frothy green gowns, none could have been happier than Kate was.

As she carefully hung the gown on the padded

hanger she had purchased just for her dress, she thought she was so lucky to finally have a glamorous, long, sparkling, beautiful gown, and at age 73 it seemed like it was about time.

Saturday,
March 29

Myrna and the Merry Widow

Myrna seemed to have no discomfort standing in the dressing room nearly naked, wearing only her panties. When Kate and Teresa arrived and she saw their surprised faces she said, "Hey, you've seen it all before, right?" She held up her bare arms and pretended to study them. "Hmmmm. Nothing new here. Hey wait, here's something new," she joked, opening her eyes very wide. "Look, it's a new wrinkle, how about that?" So they all laughed and relaxed, ready to help Myrna get into the Merry Widow and then pull on her seafoam green dress. She needed a quick costume approval from Harriet Anderson before the rest of the activities began.

Myrna held the merry widow carefully, using just her finger and thumb. "Let's see, where do we begin," she puzzled.

"Those things are made for combat," quipped Bonnie, passing by, "you don't have to treat it like cotton candy or something. Just grab it and show it who's boss."

The scholarly Olga stopped to see and couldn't resist defining it. "The Merry Widow is meant to slim your figure as long as you can stand the pure torture. It was originally designed to be a piece of armor."

Bonnie raised her hand in a victory V signal. "You see? It's made for combat!"

Olga continued. "It's a combination of a bra and a girdle, lined with long inflexible wires encased in satin ribbons which are attached to narrow panels of heavy-duty elastic and all of it comes together in a row of hooks and eyes covered by an innocent looking piece of velvet. That's the truth and you can take a teacher's word for it!"

Myrna grabbed it with both fists like an enemy. "Let's do it."

She turned around, her back facing Teresa and Kate as they took the Merry Widow and wrapped it around her, tugging and pulling it together one hook and eye at a time. Myrna held onto the back of a chair to keep steady.

Bonnie was still watching. Arms folded as she leaned against the dressing table, she asked, "Remember Lana Turner? She said this thing had to be designed by a man because a woman would never do that to another woman."

Myrna laughed, "That Lana, she sure knew a thing or two." At last, all of the hooks were fastened. She drew a big breath and stood up carefully.

Slowly she turned around so everyone could see. Bonnie, Kate, Olga, and Teresa weren't sure whether to laugh out loud or avert their eyes. "My boobs!" Myrna uttered, "where the heck did they come from?" Simple physics determine that when a

Merry Widow nips in one place, the body sticks out someplace else. And there was Myrna with a nipped in waist but her breasts flowing over the top of the Merry Widow bra.

"Come on you ladies," she ordered, "that's not what Harriet Anderson wants. She just wants to get rid of the green bra straps. We did that but now I have boobs popping out. We have to get these boobs back down where they belong!"

By now everyone was laughing. Myrna tried to stuff her overflowing breasts back into the cups of the Merry Widow. "It's not working!" she lamented. Then suddenly she had an idea. "Hey, we can just undo a few of those back hooks down at the waist. I don't need my waist cinched anyway, and that will give me a little room to tuck these boobs down below." They quickly unhooked five at the waist, and the strategy worked. Myrna had breathing room around her waist, and her bosom no longer popped out over the top.

She was ready now to slip on the dress over the Merry Widow. "Pleeeease help me get this dress on and stop all that laughing," she said in an exaggerated entreaty, fighting through the layers of seafoam green net. She raised her arms as if in prayer, closing her eyes. The strapless dress slipped easily over her head and down her torso. "Amen!" she sighed as it zipped easily up the front.

"Amen!" everyone agreed.

Myrna hurried to a mirror. "Look at that, would ya?" she said, turning around and around, admiring herself. They all smiled at her and applauded. "Hey, get your own costumes," she joked.

The rest of the dressing room was busy with everyone getting ready for gown rehearsal and approval. They fussed with their glamorous dresses, and freshened up their makeup and hair.

Harriet Anderson had posted the alphabetical order list that morning. "Ladies, you will be wearing your gowns when you present your Philosophy of Life today, and in the pageant. You will be in alphabetical order when you present your Philosophy of Life. Please be sure you know your place. We won't have time to wait around if you don't know, or while you figure out where to be."

Looking at her watch she said, "Twenty minutes, ladies. At 8:30 a.m. sharp we expect you to be on the stage, lined up in alphabetical order, looking fabulous in your gowns."

Kate, Olga, and Teresa scattered quickly to their dressing areas and prepared to put on their gowns. Myrna stayed where she was, waiting for a word from Harriet.

"Myrna, can I speak with you about your costume?" Harriet asked, motioning to her.

"Do I need the torch and the crown?" Myrna asked.

"No, I remember both of them quite well. I just want to see if the new undergarment works for you. A Merry Widow is a strange and wonderful thing, isn't it?"

Myrna turned around as Harriet watched. With a little flutter of applause, Harriet said, "Your costume looks great, Myrna. Approved."

Just before she left the dressing room she said to Myrna, in a lowered voice, "I'll be sure to get those sound guys to give you a couple more rounds with the music. I think they could use a little practice. Go get changed now. See you in a few minutes."

Getting the Gowns On

Everyone was engrossed in the business of putting on gowns. It wasn't as simple as it seemed it might be. First there were pantyhose to pull on. Most women didn't wear them anymore. Years ago they might not have stepped out without them, but these days hardly anyone wore them. "In the gown competition, everyone wears proper undergarments, including pantyhose," said Harriet Anderson. "No bare legs," she decreed.

In addition to the pantyhose, some struggled into elasticized and spandex infused bras and girdles. Strapless dresses required special undergarments. "No body parts squeezing out or flopping over," cautioned Harriet Anderson. "Not too much cleavage, cover it up. If your tummy is pooching out, put on some tight spandex or a girdle." And so it went, with groans and laughter all over the very busy room.

It was easy for Kate to slip into her Mardi Gras gown. She was fortunate to escape the strapless bras and corsets and special undergarments most of the other women struggled with, wearing only her regular bra and panties plus pantyhose. At the last

minute at home that morning she decided to pack a
black half-slip to wear under the gown. It would be
comfortable to wear a slip, and would prevent the
dreaded see-your-legs-through-your-skirt problem
which could be particularly evident under the harsh
stage lights.

While others worried about squeezing into their
gowns, Kate did not because it was her exact size,
which admittedly was not a size 2 or 4. She was well
aware that size 12 was one of the larger sizes, but it
fit her, and she just slipped it over her head, zipped
up the back and that was it. She could be dressed in
her gown in just minutes.

Which meant she had time to relax, look around
the room, and think about everything. Or rather,
think about the other women in the competition.
Shirley Mortenson had been right when she said
these were special women whose life stories were
filled with love, pain, joy, and sorrow as rich as any
she had ever known. Kate contemplated the friendships that were blooming between the women, the
care and respect they showed for each other. Kate
was honored to be connecting on some special level
with Teresa, Sherry, and Angeline but also enjoyed
the bantering friendships of Bonnie and Myrna.
Everyone loved Anita, and that was unique too
because Anita clearly loved everyone back.

Kate's thoughts came back to Teresa, Sherry,
and Angeline. She felt she could turn to them if

something arose which would require some help, understanding or support. She also felt they would turn to her in a similar situation. She pondered how and why such trust was developing but couldn't find the answer in these very few moments she had to herself. Whatever it was, she was glad for it. She pushed her chair back from the dressing table and stood up so she would be visible if one of them might be looking for her, or in case anyone at all needed assistance. The Happy Hookers had their hands full, and Kate was quite pleased to help out.

Sherry was situated in her quiet, out-of-the way corner of the room and carefully took her shimmering silver dress from the garment bag. Kate saw her thank the Happy Hooker who offered to help.

In her pale undergarments the fine wrinkles of her legs and arms were visible, like a delicate net. Her tummy had only a small pooch. Her breasts were hidden behind the molded cups of her bra but her cleavage came together in feathery wrinkles as well. After all, contestants were all age 60 and up and any examination of a face or body would show the years. Then she gently held the long silver dress on one arm. Turning away slightly from the group, she faced the shadows while she dressed.

Kate wondered if she missed joining in the fun and laughter with the rest of the women. Wasn't it ironic that she was so beautiful yet was so shy.

But then, they say Marilyn Monroe was shy too, and Sherry certainly had her beauty. Twisting her fine hair out of the way, she slipped the silver satin dress over her head and let it slide down and fall in gentle curves around her body. Her hair fell loose like a cloud around her shoulders, and it swayed as if touched by a soft breeze. Carefully she pulled pale silver satin gloves out of her suitcase and eased them over her hands and up to her elbows. With a glance at the mirror, she ran the satin gloves slowly over the dress, stopping to smooth the small shadow of her tummy.

"Could you fasten this necklace for me?" she asked the Happy Hooker, holding out a delicate chain of tiny silver roses.

"Of course," and the Happy Hooker slid the clip together. She lingered and patted Sherry's hand. It was a sweet, reassuring gesture. Kate wondered if she thought of Sherry as delicate and vulnerable too.

Sherry smiled, pale lips like pink satin and blue eyes like a summer sky. "Thank you," she whispered, and started to turn away.

The Happy Hooker lingered a moment. "You look beautiful," she said, standing back to admire her.

"Oh," Sherry whispered. It seemed to fluster her. "What's that? I'm so sorry. It's just that, well I am all ready now, thank you so much." She didn't seem to know how to finish the sentence. "Sorry."

Teresa was in another quiet area, also at the rear of the room, where she calmly undressed and slipped into her undergarments. Like Sherry, she kept her back turned and did not join the group in all the laughter, groans and jokes. She picked up her dress from a chair and looked it over before gently placing it on the floor and carefully arranging it so she could step into the center. She bent over and slowly pulled it up. It was a simple gown of white crepe, a full skirt gathered at the waist, and a bodice which gathered and covered her shoulder on one side, and was strapless on the other side. She had already fastened a small garland of turquoise flowers around her head, her wild dark hair tucked into a knot at the back of her neck with a few curls escaping.

Kate picked up a bottle of water and headed over to Teresa's area. "Hi Teresa," she said, stopping a few feet behind her, holding the water in her hand. "You remind me of a Grecian goddess."

Teresa turned around to greet Kate. "Me?" she laughed. "A Latina Grecian goddess? I don't think so." She pulled the bodice of her dress up all the way to her neck and covered her chest, not quite finished getting into the bodice. "And on top of it all, I've been reminded not to cry. A sobbing singing Latina Grecian goddess in cowboy boots," she laughed, pointing to her white cowboy boots with the gold tips which stood beside the chair. She still held the dress around her.

Just at that moment, Kate noticed Angeline wave to her from the other side of the room. "Excuse me, Teresa, I'll be right back." Kate took her water and joined Angeline.

"Could you fasten the three snaps in the back of this dress?" A long, graceful dress which exposed her back down to her waist, the dress had a halter top which closed at the back of the neck. Angeline's skin was so black it seemed to shine next to the shimmering gold gown.

"You look beautiful," Kate said, adjusting the fabric over the closure.

"Thank you," Angeline answered quietly. "Is there anything I can do to help you?" There wasn't. Kate was ready in her Mardi Gras dress and plain black pumps. She took a sip of water and looked around at the bustle of activity as everyone got ready.

It was then that Kate and some others noticed Marcia was not among them. "Where is she?" asked Jane. "I want to see the Bob Mackie designer dress she told us about."

One of the Happy Hookers looked up and answered, "She's just down the hall in the ladies room, said she would be right back. She says it is easier to get dressed where it isn't so crowded."

Suddenly the door opened and in walked Marcia, a vision in a dazzling royal purple gown of exquisite chiffon with silver beaded accents. No one said a word, they just stared. She was gorgeous! Her silver stiletto shoes were perfectly elegant, her black hair was pinned up with rhinestone clips, and her wrists glistened with sparkling bangles. "Oh," she said as if she was surprised at the stares. "I was just freshening up. Changing clothes can be so messy."

Anita broke the tension. "At least I got the right color," she laughed. Her dress was royal purple too, flecked with tiny silver dots. Anita had spent many hours sewing the dress from scratch, a flowing dress with long loose sleeves and a high empire waist.

"How pretty," Marcia said with a big smile. "It's good we won't be standing too close together."

Glancing over at Teresa, who still stood beside her chair, Kate decided to crisscross the room again to offer her help. She really didn't mind. She was having a great time prancing around in her Mardi Gras dress, thinking she would never forget the excitement of these moments. And at least her shoes were comfortable.

One look at Teresa's face told her this was something a little more serious. She doubted there would be any more joking about being a Grecian goddess or a sobbing singer. "Are you okay?" Kate asked. She had not seen such distress on Teresa's face except the morning at the kick-off meeting, when they first met and Teresa shared the memory of losing her husband.

"Sort of," Teresa answered. "I mean, yes I am okay, but can you help me with this one-shoulder thing? This is the dress my kids helped me find. I'm having trouble. Yes, let's say I'm having a challenge putting it on."

Not sure what she meant, Kate reached out to help. It didn't look complicated but Kate wanted to do whatever Teresa needed at this moment.

Teresa stopped her with a touch of her hand. "Wait. There is something I want to tell you, something I promised to explain. It seems like now is the time. I need to warn you about my scar." She paused. "Yes. My scar."

For a moment both Kate and Teresa looked into each other's eyes. Then Teresa slowly pulled the dress off her shoulder, easing it over her strapless bra. She watched to see Kate's reaction, a small widening of her eyes. "I know," she said, "it's kind of shocking. You get used to it when you see it often enough. At home I don't even think about it and neither does anyone else. When I wear a tank top everyone can see it. I don't always hide it, I don't always go around wearing a jacket. It has not seemed like the right time to show everyone in the competition. Yet. I want to show you first because I told you there were issues about getting a gown, remember that?"

Kate stared at the dark tissue which was healed but left ridges and a hollow dark depression. "Yes,

I remember. I did not know what you were talking about then. But thank you for showing me now."

"Would you like to know about it?" Teresa asked.

Kate nodded. Yes, she wanted to know about it, and she also knew that Teresa wanted to tell her. It was part of their friendship to share this moment.

Teresa explained, "It's from cancer. No, not breast cancer. Melanoma. It started out as a little mole, and I ignored it. Luis noticed it but he wasn't particularly concerned. We are ranchers, we have all sorts of dings and bruises, and a little mole did not seem very important. Then one day it started itching and I scratched it. And it got bigger. Luis noticed that too. He made me go to a doctor and the doctor did a biopsy. Cancer, he told us. Melanoma. Skin cancer, he explained, not breast cancer. I was scared to death. Luis said for me to be brave, the doctors would take care of it. They started with an incision to remove it. They thought they got it all but they didn't. In time it went into my breast and it even went down my side. I had three operations in all. First they took mostly skin tissue, then they took the whole breast, and finally they took the skin tissue down to my waist and that's what you see now. One gigantic scar where once a woman's body was whole."

Kate knew Teresa had probably explained this before. She didn't know what to say, so she waited for Teresa to continue.

"Luis was the reason I was able to go through this. He loved me no matter what. He'd look at the scar and say he didn't care. He'd say Teresa, it's you I love, a scar won't ever change that. He didn't care whether or not I had breast reconstruction either. He'd say he really didn't want me to go through more surgery, more pain and suffering. He always told me he loved me with or without a breast, with or without a scar. But Luis is gone now and I have to deal with this without him. It's okay. I'm okay. And now you know why I did not want to be in the pageant and why I did not think finding a gown would be easy."

Kate looked again at the gouged scar and felt a deep sadness. Teresa patted her arm. "Hey, like I said it's okay, Kate. My kids say so too. They are the ones who reminded me to get out here and be proud that I survived this whole thing. I was worried this scar wasn't exactly beauty pageant stuff, but they dared me to be wrong. They even contacted Best Breast Buddy to help me get a dress. It's a pretty dress, don't you think? It has a very nice prosthetic." She tugged at the bodice of her dress which was shaped with a soft and natural prosthetic.

"So here I am. Now, will you help me fit this dress over my shoulder so everyone else won't be staring at me like you are?" She smiled when she said it, and Kate knew she had trusted her to see the scar and now she wanted to get on with things. Which is exactly what they did.

"Okay, that should do it," Kate said as she zipped up the side of the white dress. She gave Teresa a quick hug. "Thank you for telling me, for trusting me," she said. They hugged again and hurried to join the other women who were walking out of the dressing room in their beautiful gowns.

Modeling the Gowns

"My goodness, you all look so lovely!" said Harriet Anderson as the candidates filed onto the stage in their gowns, and of course everyone applauded.

"Let me begin by telling you that we have a Master of Ceremonies for our pageant. Many of you will know him – he is Charlie O'Day. He has been on the radio for years, a talk show host. This will be his fifth year as our MC, and our audiences always love him. Be sure to introduce yourself the night of the pageant, although he will be very busy keeping things moving in the show.

"We've also chosen the judges for the pageant. It's very exciting! They are excited and we are excited. The five judges will remain anonymous until the night before the pageant when you will meet them for your interview. We will get to that part later. For now, I want to assure you that the judges are all well-known and respected members of our community. They are not associated with this pageant in any way. They are not former Queens or contestants. They are not sponsors or donors. They are people who we feel are qualified to select the best among you to be Queen.

"Here is how those judges will choose the Queen. It may not seem too complicated but as you will see, there is more to it than just numbers. But let's start with the numbers. The judges will be given score sheets with four areas to score. Each area is worth a certain percent of the total score:

Philosophy of Life	20%
Gown	30%
Talent	30%
Interview	20%
TOTAL	**100%**

"If only it were that simple, but of course it is not quite so cut and dry. While they are scoring they will be influenced by many other things related to these areas. Let's think about them. Your smile. How you relate to the audience. How poised you are on the stage and in interviews. Your self-confidence. Your grace. There is more, of course, but you can be sure that every single thing you do from the moment they meet you will be watched and evaluated. It may not turn up as a score by itself, but it will have an impact on the scores they award to you.

"Now we can get started practicing what you do on the stage while you wear your beautiful gowns. As you know, you wear them during the presentation of your Philosophy of Life, but there is more to it than that. Today we will show you how to model your gown."

She smiled and looked up and down the line of women. "You didn't think you would just walk around the stage any which way at all, did you? Of course not! That's why you will learn to model your gown.

"We want you to look and be your very best when you introduce yourself. You will be wearing your gown when you walk on stage to say your name, age and city. Starting at that moment, your gown and how you wear it is 30% of your score, ladies. Thirty percent!

"Then you will present your Philosophy of Life. That Philosophy of Life will account for 20% of your total score, ladies. Twenty percent!

"Add it up, ladies. Your gown plus your Philosophy of Life. Together, these two equal a total of 50% of your score. Fifty percent!"

"You will get some good practice in your gown today, but you will probably want to practice some more. I strongly recommend you wear your gown at home while you practice your Philosophy of Life. Wear it to practice how to walk to one side of the stage, turn around, walk to the other side of the stage and turn around, all the while smiling and looking beautiful and poised like a Queen!

"We will go through this now so you get the idea. You can ask questions as we go along. You can take notes if you wish. Then we will go through everything a second time. Finally, you will do it completely on your own. That third time? No questions. No notes. Just do it.

"Everyone please make your way to the back curtain, line up behind it. Remain lined up in alphabetical order by last name. You've done this before. You will walk to the microphone, just like before, and give your name, age and city, wait for applause, and then give your Philosophy of Life, just like before. But this time, you will be modeling."

Anita turned and started toward the back of the stage. She carried her shoes in one hand, and Harriet Anderson took notice. "Anita! I can't believe you have your shoes off again. At this point you simply must wear your shoes all the time, with the one exception of when you actually sit down to play the piano. Go back to where we were and put them on. You are modeling. You are not a barefoot model. I really don't want to mention this again." Anita looked embarrassed as she made her way back to a chair where she could sit and put on her shoes.

Everyone else walked to the back of the stage, a familiar walk they had taken many times now. Kate wore her plain black shoes. Myrna wore her patent leather platform boots – she never did purchase any high heels, insisting that the boots would hardly show under the dress anyway.

Bonnie wore thick, six-inch tall platform heels in Regal Gold. "What else would a Queen wear, for crying out loud? Did you think I was going to wear Mildred's shoes?"

Teresa wore her white high heeled cowboy boots with gold tips. Helen's shoes were black with burgundy flowers at the toe, a perfect match for her gown of deep burgundy with black lace. Olga's were delicate, almost invisible with tiny silver ribbons wrapped around her feet and ankles, a far cry from the sturdy clogging shoes she wore for her talent. Marcia's were the prettiest of all, smooth silver leather across the instep, tall and sleek crystal stiletto heels, small rhinestone flowers on one side. Anita caught up wearing her sparkling silver shoes and this time she made no clever comments as she walked to the back of the stage.

"While I describe the modeling technique, former Queen Shirley Mortenson will demonstrate for you," said Harriet. Shirley stood at the very front of the line, just ahead of Anita. "When I call Shirley's name, she will step forward and wave." She did. "She will smile." She was already smiling. "She will walk forward to the microphone, stop and smile." She was still smiling. "Say her name, age, city, and she will wait for the audience to applaud." She did, and the audience applauded. "Now she will recite her Philosophy of Life." She didn't, but it was clear what

Harriet meant and she went on, "The audience will applaud again" – they did – "and she will smile." She did.

"Now, here is where the modeling begins. Shirley, please take one step sideways to the right side of the microphone so everyone can see how lovely you look in your gown. Wait there for a few seconds. Don't wave, don't bow, don't curtsy, just wait. And smile. Now, walk to the far right corner at the front of the stage. Head up! Back straight! Slowly, don't rush. Smile! Ladies, watch carefully to see where Shirley is going. And notice, Shirley is smiling at the audience the whole way.

"At that far end, please pause and smile. Big smile! The photographer will be there to take your picture. Snap. Now walk to the center of the stage, stop and look at the audience. Smile, then turn around, face back, turn around and face the audience again. It's called a pivot. One full turn. Smile.

"Now Shirley, please walk all the way across the front to the other end of the stage. Ladies, the judges will be seated in the first row on that side. Look at the judges and smile." She did.

"Turn and let the judges see the back of your gown. Pivot and face front again. Smile. Turn around one last time. There will be a gentleman in a tuxedo, we don't know who he will be yet, but he will take your arm and escort you off the stage."

Shirley left the stage holding the arm of the stage hand, who stood in for the gentlemen in the tuxedo. Both of them waved. Everyone applauded.

"Thank you so much, Shirley. Now, would you please return to the front of the line and do the whole thing one more time? I will talk you through it again, just to be sure everyone understands." One more time, Shirley demonstrated how to model and make an impact wearing the gown.

"It's your turn now," said Harriet, turning to the ladies standing in line at the back of the stage. Anita Archer. You are first."

Anita smiled, "Of course! First in alphabetical order. First in performance order. Hey, First Place?" she joked as she stepped forward.

The practice continued through the morning with only one short break. It was a very long two hour rehearsal in glamorous gowns and glorious high heels.

As the practice ended, some of the women turned to go to the dressing room. "I can't wait to get out of these shoes," groaned Anita. It was the common complaint of most of the others, too.

"I know you are tired," said Harriet, "but we are not finished. Not yet. Everyone keep your shoes on." She glanced sternly at Anita. "Keep your gowns on too." It was a joke. "Keep smiling. Stay tuned. There is more fun to follow."

Gown Photos

Kate felt drained after standing in her heels for almost two hours. Even her sensible black shoes had their limit. She couldn't wait for the modeling practice to end so she could take off her shoes, sit down, and relax. But there was one more thing to do before Harriet excused everyone and they could rush back to the comfort of the dressing room. Gown photos. Dave had his camera equipment set up and ready to go.

Kate was not the only one feeling the pain of the shoes. "Who would think some little ribbons could be so painful," moaned Olga. "It's like walking on tip toe for the last two hours. My feet are screaming."

Anita groaned, "Like I said, it's a good thing I play the piano and don't have to dance."

Marcia seemed to have a system of rocking from one foot to the other on her tall stilettos, but even she commented, "These shoes are meant to be seen, not for standing in for hours on end." Admiring the beautiful shoes, Kate could not help but agree.

"Everyone please move forward for the camera," Harriet said. "This time you will stand arranged by height. Tallest women please stand in the center, shortest at the ends." This meant, of course, that Anita stood in the center, all 5' 10" of her plus her high heels, Bonnie stood next to her perched in her Regency Gold platforms, Marcia stood halfway down on the left side, Kate was halfway down on the right side. Teresa and Myrna were at the ends. For that moment, in their beautiful gowns, it didn't seem to matter where anyone was placed. Harriet walked down the line of women, all of them dressed so elegantly, and looked carefully at each dress, smiling and nodding at each one. "Lovely," she said, "just lovely. Please stay where you are and let Dave take his photos."

Everyone smiled royally for the camera. Only one woman would be Queen, but at that moment all of them were Queens. "Beautiful!" said the photographer, snapping several shots.

For just a fleeting moment, standing beneath the stage lights with her new hair style and makeup, and wearing the glamorous sparkling gown, Kate thought of Jim. For the briefest of moments Kate wondered what he would think of her, the most glamorous she had ever been. Would he even know who she was? Or did he still think of her as she was back then, just as she thought of him? After all this time, all their life experiences, they were not the same two young lovers they were all those years ago. But he was there in her memory once again and at this moment Kate thought so very fondly of him, again. She wondered what had prompted her nostalgia. Was it Teresa and how she missed her Luis? Was it Myrna and Harold's fierce devotion? Was it Anita and Mr. Nick? She wasn't sure, but then it really didn't matter. "Dear Jim," she thought. But only for a moment.

Dave waved and announced, "We have some really nice shots here. Thanks everyone, I am done for the day."

Harriet thanked him and said, "I can't wait to see your wonderful photos."

To the ladies she said, "It's time to change clothes again. You've got thirty minutes. The luncheon begins at 12:00 noon. It's good practice, you need to be able to change quickly on the day of the pageant."

She held up her hand, a signal for everyone to stop one more time. "Oh! And by the way, all of your gowns are approved. Every single one of them. Congratulations!

"See you shortly, everyone. No time to waste."

Everyone Has a Story

The first thing Kate did when she got to the dressing room was kick off her plain black shoes. She fell into her chair at the dressing table and massaged her throbbing feet, all the while groaning with relief. She was not alone. The room resonated with groans and moans as every woman removed her shoes. It had been a long morning on their feet, and Harriet Anderson said it was good practice. "Good practice for a torture chamber," said Bonnie.

Standing in her bare feet, Kate unzipped the Mardi Gras gown and slipped it onto the padded hanger. She appreciated walking barefoot across the cool floor, wiggling her toes in continued relief from the marathon in the high heels. Carefully, she hung the gown on the dress rack. She enjoyed wearing it, but it was heavy and warm and she was glad to take it off now. She changed into her beige sweater and dark gray slacks. Not ready to put on her flat shoes yet, she left them on the floor beside the chair.

Angeline had also changed her clothes and stood barefoot as she folded her gold gown. She placed it in her suitcase, then sighed softly as she sat down and relaxed. Kate thought Angeline might say something about her aching feet too, but instead she leaned back in her chair and said, "The pageant is better this year than it was last year, especially the talent. Last year the talent was not as interesting."

Kate stretched out her legs and looked at Angeline. "Last year? You mean this is your second time in the pageant?"

"Oh no, not my second time," said Angeline. Last year I watched the pageant but I was not in it. I am comparing what I saw last year to this year." She nodded toward Olga. "She has been in the pageant twice before. A candidate is permitted to compete in the pageant three times, so this is her final try. Her clogging has improved so much! She makes it very entertaining. You've seen how much fun it is, haven't you? She works very hard for this. I hope she does well this time."

"Was her talent the same last year as it is this year?" Kate asked.

"I suppose. It was clogging," Angeline answered, "but it was different. This year she changed the music and her costume. She says she has learned a lot about how to perform, write a good philosophy, and choose a good gown. She thinks even the shoes matter, and this year she has those delicate little ribbon shoes to prove it. Hopefully she's found the things the judges like. That is how she prepared for this year."

It had never occurred to Kate that anyone would

enter more than one time. She had not even thought about using the experience one year to build on a performance for the following year. "Tell me about what you learned from watching it last year," she asked.

"For me, because I am a singer, I learned that the choice of a song is very important. More than I knew. I have had a lot of help from my singing coach." She smiled and explained, "Singing is one of my biggest pleasures. I've been taking lessons twice a month from a teacher in Pendleton. I am a far better singer now than I was a year ago. Back then I sang mostly for fun."

Angeline was not one to rush anything, and it was a few seconds before she continued. "It has to be a certain kind of song, something the judges feel is worthy of a Queen. It has to be a song that they really like for its character, and it has to suit you somehow, whether it is a blues song or a love song, that's the trick. The song I chose, "Unforgettable," seems like a good choice. We shall see."

"I learned that the style of dress you choose, the jewelry you wear makes an impression on the judges too. I am still learning. This is just my first try, the first time I have actually competed in the pageant. I am doing my best, but mostly I am watching and listening and learning. I want to be Queen, but right now I want to learn what it takes to be Queen. I am grateful for all of the help I am getting."

There were still a few minutes until the noon luncheon, and Kate looked around the room, thinking about the variety of talent among the contestants. A quick tally showed that eleven of the sixteen were singers and dancers. The five who were not were Anita, who played the piano; Bonnie, a comedian; Rosemarie, an actress; Sandi, a magician; and Kate, who recited poetry. The rest were singers and dancers, which made sense, as these were talents that many women cultivated as girls and continued throughout their lives. Singers and dancers often made it to the top five of pageant talent. A really good singer might go far. One old Queen had been a front singer for a local band and really knew how to belt out the blues. In the year she competed, she not only became Ms. Senior Tri-Rivers but also made it to first runner up at the national competition. The other successful talent, dancing, also held a lot of promise. It seems in addition to hearing a good song, the judges liked to see a little leg, a lot of movement, and great smiles. Last year's winner of Ms. Senior Tri-Rivers was a dancer. A very good dancer, they emphasized, but then does anyone win who is not very good?

What about those whose talent was neither of these? How did they fare? "A monologue is just fine, although I can't think of anyone who has ever won the title of Ms. Senior Tri-Rivers with a monologue,"

Shirley Mortenson said early on when she discussed Kate's decision to recite poetry as her talent. She may have had second thoughts because she quickly added, "But there is always a first time!"

Was it only singers and dancers who won? Had a comedian ever won, or an actress, Kate wanted to know. "Oh yes, there have been winners who weren't singers or dancers," declared Shirley. Kate asked who and when. Once again Shirley pondered the question and could not remember exactly who or when. It really didn't make any difference, Kate decided, because the results of this pageant would be decided in just a few days, and the odds were pretty good it would be a singer or a dancer.

Thinking of the patience and practice it required to prepare, Kate turned to Angeline and said, "This pageant must mean a lot to you, to go about it this way."

She nodded, "Yes, it is my dream to be Ms. Senior Tri-Rivers. It has been my goal for a while. Having goals is very important to me. I always have a goal." She had been just a girl in South Africa, she told Kate, when she realized that the United States of America was good, very good, and she wanted to live here. She set her first goal: someday she would find a way to get to the United States and if she could, she would bring her family too. The years passed and she kept the dream in her mind, working hard in school and doing what she could to help her family. "I was the oldest girl. I had to help a lot."

After she completed year eight of standard school – the last and final year available to young black girls if they could go at all – she got a job and took a bus into Johannesburg early each morning and worked by day as a housekeeper. At night she returned to the crowded home where she helped prepare dinner and took care of the smaller children.

"I was just seventeen when a family from the United States, the Cabots, came to visit my employer in Johannesburg as houseguests. They liked me and offered me a job in their home in Chicago. I would take care of the house cleaning and their flower garden, and help with other things. I hoped I could save some money and someday bring my family to the United States too, so I accepted their offer.

"The Cabots were very kind to me and helped me get more schooling. In South Africa my education ended, and apartheid made it impossible to get more schooling because that was for white people. In the United States I soon made new goals. First I would work hard to become a citizen. They helped me, and on my 19th birthday I took my oath of allegiance and became a citizen of the United States of America.

"Another goal was to bring my family here one day. I began to save my money. About that time I met a nice older gentleman, Mr. Schneider, a banker who

helped me to open my savings account. I decided that
working in a bank would be a good job for me, and
it became my next goal. I studied hard and learned
math and accounting so I could be hired as a bank
clerk. About that time, Mr. Schneider was promoted
to be a bank manager in Pendleton, and he and his
family moved. He told me if I ever wanted to come to
work for him, he would find me a job. My employers,
the Cabots, gave me a good reference, and Mr.
Schneider hired me and that is how I came to live
in the Tri-Rivers. I told you, the United States of
America is the very best place in the world."

Fascinated, Kate did not notice Harriet
Anderson enter the dressing room, but Angeline did.
"Ladies," Harriet asked, "will you join us now for
lunch?"

They wiggled their toes one more time before
they stood up, put on their shoes, and started toward
the door. "I'd love to hear the rest of your story,
Angeline," Kate said. "Can we talk some more later?"

Angeline nodded. "Of course. Do you have time
after the luncheon, or is that too much for one day?"

With Lolita happily cared for the rest of the day,
Kate could not think of anything she would rather
do. "Meet you outside after the luncheon," she said.

Getting to Know You Luncheon

Clusters of blue and white balloons and purple ribbons decorated the far end of the Performance Hall lobby. "Over here, ladies. The luncheon is right down here," directed the hostesses. Folding chairs and tables were arranged in a circle so that everyone could see each other. White tablecloths, lavender paper napkins, silver and blue paper flower center-pieces, and white paper plates adorned the small tables. Blue name tags were on each of the eight tables, two candidates and one old Queen per table.

After the candidates found their seats, Harriet Anderson tapped her spoon on the table to get every-one's attention. "Welcome!" she said enthusiastically. "We are so proud of you and everything you have accomplished, and we are so happy to have you as our guests at this luncheon." Aglow in her long blue pageant gown and white sash, she also wore huge sapphire earrings and a matching necklace for the special occasion. Behind her stood a row of old Queens, the hosts of the luncheon, all dressed in their finery too. Harriet took a moment to introduce them.

The Age of Elegance

They all smiled and waved except the rascally old Eleanor Butler who kept her cane firmly in hand and firmly planted on the floor.

Harriet reminded everyone that the lunch was a special opportunity for the candidates to informally tell a little bit about themselves. There were two suggested topics for the candidates: tell us something about yourself we might not know, and, tell us why you decided to be in this pageant.

Not everyone had been comfortable with the idea, but at least they had fair warning and also wanted to hear what the others had to say. The last line of the invitation read, "It is good practice to talk about yourself. You must be able to talk to people wherever you go, and they will ask you many things. So go ahead and think about the above questions and when we call on you at the luncheon just relax and tell us about yourself."

At the side of the lobby was a long table with trays of sandwiches, fruits and veggies, chips and dip, and chocolate chip cookies. Coffee urns and cups were on a separate table. "Please serve yourself lunch, then we will begin the program" said a handwritten, folded table tent. Harriet invited everyone to stand up and serve themselves.

Anita Archer raised her hand. "Harriet, before we begin may I ask everyone to join hands in prayer? We have a lot to be thankful for today, would that be all right?"

Harriet Anderson looked around the group and seeing that everyone was already standing and starting to join hands, she said, "Of course. Anita, will you lead us?"

Anita lowered her head and prayed, "Lord, we thank you for the privilege of being here together with each other, for the good food we are about to receive, for the bounty of friendship and love among us, and for watching over us. Please bless us and keep us forever and ever. Amen."

Anita looked up and asked, "Would anyone else like to offer a prayer?"

Without missing a beat, 87-year-old Eleanor Butler raised her hand and shouted, "And we all say Halleluiah and Amen!" And everyone let go of each other's hands and picked up their plates and headed for the food.

Myrna was the first one to reach the table and quickly filled her plate. Balancing it in one hand, she moved to the other table, reached for the coffee urn and filled her cup. Picking it up, she did not realize how hot it was and with an instinctive reflex she dropped the cup. "Ow!" she yelped. The cup fell to the table then bounced to the floor, the hot coffee splattering everywhere. As the coffee splashed onto her leg, she dropped her plate full of food and it flew everywhere too.

Marcia was standing right behind Myrna.

Reacting instantly, her hands flew protectively out in front of her. "Oh no," she yelled, "Not on my cashmere sweater!" She jumped sideways quickly to escape the spatter of food and coffee and turned to make a hasty escape. Myrna, covered with spilled food and coffee and visibly distressed, bent over and tearfully repeated, "I am so sorry!" The floor was wet and messy as she moaned, "Oh no!" trying to pick up the food.

As quickly as Marcia escaped, Angeline rushed forward from about half-way down the line to help Myrna, first putting her arm around her asking, "Are you okay? Don't worry, this is nothing, let me help." The coffee and food spilled onto Angeline's dress, but she paid no attention to that.

Right behind her was Helen, soothing Myrna and using a napkin to wipe the coffee from Myrna's clothes, saying "It's okay, it's okay." Carol and Stephanie grabbed a handful of the lavender napkins and wiped up the floor, while Judith pulled over a trash can. Kate and the others at the rear of the line just tried to just stay out of the way of the five who were already helping. Kate was sure there were others who would have helped too, but wasn't it just like these five to be there first, caring, soothing, helping? That, she thought, is a noble trait, a special talent. But of course there is nowhere for that on the score card of a judge.

Marcia found a seat at the rear of the hall where she was able to check her sweater and skirt for spots of coffee or food as she waited. When everything calmed down she stood up and stepped back in line. "I'll just have something to drink," she said, avoiding the table with the stains from the spill.

When everyone was seated at the tables, Harriet took charge of the luncheon program once again. "Thank you everyone for helping us get through this little accident. Don't give it another thought, Myrna, everyone is okay, everything is fine, so now let us begin our program. Feel free to enjoy your food and beverages as we continue."

Looking expectantly at the group, she stated, "Now it is time for each of you to tell us about you. Say whatever you wish, just relax and feel comfortable because however you answer the questions is strictly up to you. This is just for fun. No judges, no score."

She turned to the table closest to her and said, "Sandi? We'll start with you. Please introduce yourself the same way you introduce yourself when you do your Philosophy of Life: Name. Age. City. Then go ahead and tell us about yourself."

"Oh my gosh," said Sandi, standing up and looking around the room. "I didn't expect to be the first one. Usually it's Anita. Okay, well, Sandi Meredith. 62. East Mercer City. My husband Tom and I both grew up in Colorado. We learned the real estate and mortgage business there. We moved here years ago and decided we should start our own business and we like to think that after all these years we are now the premiere mortgage brokers for all of the Tri-Rivers area. We named our business, Meredith Mortgage, pretty straight forward, and I hope you've heard of us. Being married to the man I work with means he can never say he is the boss. He'd say the same thing about being married to me. We are partners in our business, both of us do all the work, both of us are the boss!

"We have three kids, all grown and gone with homes of their own. Being in the mortgage business, they better have homes of their own, right? Our life is pretty normal. We have dinner parties sometimes, and that is where I got the idea for my talent, thinking it would be great fun sometime to spice up our own dinner parties with some magic. Well, I hardly ever get to do it at home but it sure is fun to give it a try here. I am still working on that disappearing knife trick. Tom says just don't practice it in the office. Bad for business. I'll get it right the night of the show. Why am I in the pageant? To get away from the office, of course!"

"Thank you, Sandi. That wasn't so bad, was it? I see you are still smiling. So let's carry on with the next person." Harriet nodded at Bonnie, saying "that would be you."

Bonnie stood up and said, "Would you believe I am not just another pretty face? Oh yes, and I am Bonnie Gabriel. 64. Pendleton. I actually have a profession – I make wedding cakes. It's funny the things you do when you are divorced. And I bet you all know who I was married to, right? Come on, with my last name? Gabriel? Do any of you watch Channel 14 news? Ever heard of Clark Gabriel? News Anchor? For real, Clark Gabriel. What famous movie star do you think his mom had in mind when she named him Clark Gabriel? Yep, he's the guy I was married to, as in 'was' until he got in the habit of taking up with one little weather girl after another when he got promoted to the evening news twenty years ago. He's a lot older now – aren't we all – but the weather girls are still young and he keeps trying. I still use his famous last name. Thank God we never had kids, and they don't have to explain that name. Being in the wedding cake business people do a double take. But you know how it is. Everything is coming up roses when you are getting married, right? What could ever go wrong? Ha! I have to say, being the character 'Mildred' is perfect for me. I just use my real life experience to put together my act. So now you know all about me. I hope I will be on Channel 14 news. See Ms. Senior Tri-Rivers. See Clark Gabriel freak out! As Mildred would say, I'm a lot more delicious than I look."

Without waiting to be asked, Olga stood up and introduced herself. She knew she was next. "Olga Asamova. 64. Mercer City. I wonder if any of you know that there is a direct correlation between dancing and math? And playing the piano and math? It's true. If you have ability for one you often have ability for the other. So as a child I excelled at math. I was a math champion by the sixth grade and went on to get a scholarship to college primarily because of my math ability. And I studied some piano, but certainly never got to the level of Anita Archer. And fortunately, my parents enrolled me in clogging classes and lo and behold I could dance. So don't laugh when you see me out there clogging away. There is a math whiz out there too. Seriously, I have been a math teacher most of my life. My husband Arthur is a teacher too. He teaches biology, not math. He and I got together – you know, math and biology – and got married and had a couple of kids, a boy and a girl, and neither of them is talented at all in either math or biology. Go figure. But they think it's great that I am competing for Ms. Senior Tri-Rivers, and so do the grandkids, who are also quite clever at math. They always say, "Do the math, Grandma!" I am not quite sure what they mean, but this is the third time –one-two-three – I have entered the pageant and maybe they mean the third time is the charm. Maybe the odds are finally with me and

I hope I will be the first dancing mathematic Ms. Senior Tri-Rivers."

"Thank you, Olga. Let's go to the next person. Angeline, that will be you."

Looking around the room at everyone, she seemed to wait for exactly the right moment to say, "Angeline Zolta. 62. Pendleton. I was born in Soweto, South Africa. Soweto is short for South Western Township, the name of a sprawling area southwest of Johannesburg, a place strewn with shelters made from cardboard boxes or scraps of wood and metal. When I was growing up there, the dirt streets were always dusty, there were no trees, no relief from the sun and the heat, and there were just a few tiny shops and street vendors, their wares always plagued with flies. I would say it was a place of mostly misery. I was born the year after apartheid began and black people were forced to live apart from white people who lived in the city. Black people could work for the white people, but they had to live in places like Soweto. I guess the thing you might not know about me is that I found a way to leave South Africa and become an American citizen many years ago. I want you to know how wonderful it is to be a citizen of this country. How privileged I am and you are to be here, to live here, to work here, to be in this pageant. I would be so proud to be Ms. Senior Tri-Rivers, because being an American citizen is the most important thing I can say about myself. I am an American. Now you know that about me."

Suddenly Anita pushed back her chair, jumped up, rushed over and grabbed Angeline in a big hug. "We are all Americans!" she gushed. "God bless America!" What else could everyone do at such a moment? They applauded.

"All right then, let's continue with the other ladies," said Harriet Anderson. "Sherry? You are next."

"Hi everyone. Isn't this nice?" she said, in her delicate way, dressed in a pale blue flowered blouse and white pants. "I am Sherry Springfield. 66. South Mercer City. And I have something for you, Harriet."

Sherry walked to the windows at the side of the lobby where she had placed a tall glass vase filled with pink roses. A pink satin ribbon with a big bow was tied around it. She picked up the vase and carried it to Harriet, saying, "Thank you for all you do for us."

Harriet was speechless. Bonnie couldn't resist. "I think this is the only time we will ever see Harriet speechless," she said, and everyone laughed. Harriet accepted the vase of roses, took a big breath of their fragrance, and when she looked up there might have been tears in her eyes.

Sherry continued. "I was thinking all of you know that I sing. But probably most of you don't know I raise roses, all different kinds. I love working outside in the summer, taking care of my roses. My husband, his name is Danny, he built me a greenhouse after he retired and didn't have to travel any more. I think he felt guilty for all the years he had to be away for work and wanted to make it up to me. Now I raise roses almost all year round, and it is my very favorite place to be. Except here, of course, because this is something I have really wanted to do. To sing on stage again. I was trained as an opera singer back in my college days. I attended Arizona State University School of Musical Arts and performed in several light opera productions with the Lyric Opera Theatre. I kept singing after I graduated, then Danny and I got married and I still tried to sing as much as I could while being a wife and raising our two girls. You all know how that goes. Most of it was my responsibility. Music has meant so much to me all of my life. Even these days, when I am in the greenhouse I usually have a CD playing and I sing along. So, while I still sing, this may be the last time I have the chance to sing in front of an audience, something I have wanted to do so very much. Thank you all for your patience with me. Sorry if I seem shy." She paused, as if not certain how to continue, then went on, "I am having such a lovely time. It is like a dream, raising my roses and singing."

Everyone smiled at the pretty woman who seemed so shy. Kate couldn't help but think of the beautiful roses Sherry grew, and how much like a rose she was. And she wondered what Sherry meant about "the last time I have a chance to sing" and what it was she was just about to say, but didn't.

"Thank you, Sherry. The roses are so lovely. Anita, it looks like you are next. All right everyone, here is Anita Archer."

"Anita Archer. 68. Colby. Look at that, I started the way I am supposed to. For once I got it right. And I have my shoes on, too," she smiled. "I guess you might think I am an open book, you might think there isn't much about me that you don't already know – but I have a surprise for you. I am going to share something you would have no idea about. Did you know that my Daddy owned a hardware store? Well, when I was a little girl he gave me a saw. A plain old saw. He said to me, Anita, this is just a plain old saw. But we are going to make beautiful music with this saw. And he sat me down, and he showed me how. So today I am going to show you what he showed me."

Anita pulled out a long saw from a big satchel at the side of her table. The satchel had gone unnoticed because there were so many bags and suitcases carried by the contestants. No one paid any notice to the bag, and no one knew there was a saw in the bag.

Anita held it up to show to everyone.

"Here's my saw. You start by holding it up close to you. Then you bend it, twist it, and flex until it makes a sound of its own. Next you grab a bow. We made our own bow from a yardstick and some fishing line. You grab that bow and stroke it over the saw. There you have it, as pretty a tune as you will ever hear, and it came from nothing fancy. My Daddy told me to always remember that the simplest things can surprise you, whether they are tools or people. I guess you could say that I am a simple person, but I hope I surprised you today."

As Anita sat down and put her saw back in the satchel, Marcia stood up and stepped behind her chair. With her hands resting easily on the back of the chair she introduced herself.

"Marcia Van Horne. 63. Devonville." Marcia smiled her pageant smile. Everything seemed so easy for her, even the smiling. "How nice, Anita, to share that with us. Imagine playing a saw – it is definitely a surprise. Now, I just want to be sure I answer the question, which was, 'What is something you might not know about me?' Well that's a bit difficult because there are so many things that I've been involved in. Let's see, I grew up in Philadelphia and developed a huge interest in art when I went to a boarding school that emphasized fine arts. My parents were very involved in the arts, and they wanted the same thing for me. So I guess one thing you might not know is that with my background, I was able to become the Chair of the Modern Art Museum Auxiliary Board. Modern art is my favorite genre. To me it is very similar to jazz dancing. Both of them are so free and yet so disciplined.

"My husband Chad is an attorney specializing in international law. He retired a few years ago but he is well known, and we still travel all over the world. Actually we were married only three years ago because before that I was so busy with my career I just did not have time. Now we go to museums and meet the directors, tell them about the Modern Art Museum and my volunteer work on the Board. Like I say in my philosophy of life, I am always in pursuit of my goals, whether it is a chairmanship or Ms. Senior Tri-Rivers, which I have set as one of my goals and which I hope very much to be."

"Thank you," said Harriet. "Myrna, will you go next?"

With a big grin Myrna stood up and said, "Hey Marcia, you should come to New York! They have some great art there. Oh yea, let me tell you who I am, although I think you already know. Myrna Brenner. 75. Northridge. For me, in all of my life I never had such a nice job as being an elevator girl in New York City back in 1955. I was young, just finished high school. We wore gray suits, a little gray hat, white gloves. Every day I would starch and press my white cotton blouse so it would look crisp and nice under my jacket. Then one day they told all of us that they weren't going to use elevator girls any more. We lost our jobs. They were going to change the elevators, take out the big brass levers we used to open and close the doors and all, they were going to put in buttons for every floor and let everyone push the buttons themselves. Times had changed. I had to find another job, working as a waitress and so on. In a couple of years I ended up getting married, having kids, working in a bar for a while, you know how it goes when you are getting by. I got married more than once, and divorced more than once too. Ha Ha! I always wished I could to do something nice like when I was that elevator operator.

"Anyway, after I retired and all, one night I was in a Karaoke Bar – I always liked to sing – I was singing "New York, New York" and this guy says to me I should be Miss New York. Well, I told him we aren't in New York any more, last time I looked. But the guy says to me, it was Harold who said it, well maybe you should be in this pageant they were talking about on a TV program or something. So he called the TV station and found out about it. It's Harold who thought I should be Ms. Senior Tri-Rivers and so here I am. And it turns out, it is one of the nicest things I have ever done. Hey, and thanks everyone for being so nice about the accident. It is a great lunch, I hate to waste a bite of it!"

Harriet waited for Myrna to sit down then asked, "Teresa, are you ready to go next?" Teresa nodded and stood up, her cowboy jacket buttoned at her waist. She tugged slightly at the hem of the jacket, then looked around the room, ready to speak.

"Hi everyone, Teresa Rodriguez. 61. Grover Plains. I think most of you know I am kind of a cowgirl, I mean I live on a little ranch called *Rancho Rico*, drive a truck and wear boots and jeans. I've lived on a ranch most of my life and spent a lot of time outside. And like most cowgirls, I like the sun. That's the problem, and that's what you might not know about me. There was a time when I wore tank tops and bathing suits out in the sun, riding my horse, whatever. Didn't we all dress like that when we were young? For me there was a deadly conse-quence. Melanoma. Yes, skin cancer. It started when I was about 45 years old. I developed a tiny little mole on my chest, just above my breast. I ignored it, and Luis, my husband, did too. Then one day it itched and I scratched it. And it got bigger. Luis noticed it and made me go to a doctor about it. The doctor did a biopsy. I was scared to death. Cancer, he told us. Skin cancer, not breast cancer. Melanoma. Well, to get to the point it required three operations over a few years to get rid of it. Three operations that destroyed a lot of skin and tissue and my breast, leaving one gigantic scar where once a woman's body was whole."

Kate noticed those were the very same words Teresa said to her.

"I'm taking off my jacket so I can show you how it all ended, or at least some of the scar. Don't worry, I'm leaving on my tank top. I went through a lot, but my husband helped me and encouraged me through it all. He was my biggest supporter. He saw my body change and never stopped loving me. It made no difference to him, and I hope it won't make any difference to you either. I am a survivor, just like all of you. We women of the age of elegance are all survivors. We have all experienced pain and sorrow, we all got through life to this point and all of us bear scars. This is mine. This, and the loss of my beloved husband, Luis. So now you know, and you don't need to look away or wonder about the scar. It's just who I am."

Anita Archer, a full head taller than Teresa, rushed in and swept Teresa into a big hug and whirled her around. "We love you just exactly the way you are," she exclaimed before putting Teresa down. Everyone in the room was laughing now, as Teresa hugged Anita back. Kate wiped the tears from her eyes. She was glad she already knew, otherwise she might have left the room bawling.

"May I put your jacket on the back of your chair?" said Harriet Anderson, straightening it out as she did. "We have to move on to the next person. Judith Ann, that's you."

"Judith Ann Cole. 69. Clarksdale. I believe I have more children and grandchildren in my family than any of you. Did any of you know that? I am blessed to be the proud mother of four boys, one of them died at a very young age, and four girls, and grandmother of 17. Yes, 17. You might have guessed we are Mormon. We are hardy people and have lived through a lot, but here is something I am pretty sure you wouldn't know. My great grandparents were polygamists. It's true, and although my Great-Grandpa had three wives, lots of men had more than he did. When they settled here in the Tri-Rivers, they felt it was their duty to populate, and they did a great job. The Cole family is a pretty big family, I can tell you there are a whole lot of cousins and aunts and uncles out there with the Cole name. We stick together as a family, especially when we have hard times. I couldn't have gotten by without my family when we lost our son, or when I injured my back. This cane was hand made for me by Uncle Phinnius Cole. But back to polygamy. We Mormons did away with polygamy a long while ago. Needless to say, my husband Arnie and I are not polygamists but we are devout Mormons and I praise God for the opportunity to be here in this pageant with all of you. That's why I wrote the song I am performing. To praise God."

"Thank you, Judith Ann. Seventeen grandchildren?" Harriet sighed. "I can barely cope with three. Now let's hear from Jane Morrison."

"Jane Morrison. 63. Mercer City. Gosh, I am not anything special like all of you, but I am here in the pageant because it just looked like so much fun and my friends thought I should do it. I live a pretty ordinary life, you know how it goes. I got married to my high school sweetheart Scott when we were just 19, and he worked in his father's auto shop all these years, and we had kids, raised them and life was good. But instead of being free as a bird when our kids were gone, all of a sudden Scott's dad had a heart attack and died and Scott took over the whole shop, and his Mom was all alone and needed help. And then my Mom got sick and Dad needed to take care of her and he was having a hard time, so I started helping them too and it seemed like I never had time for anything else. And as if that was not enough, I started getting pain in my hands and my knees and the doctor said, Jane, that's arthritis. You need to start exercising. So one day I noticed there was a Dancing Queen exercise class in the social room at my church. I tried it out, and it was so much fun that I started going three times a week. That's where I learned all my dance moves. Heck, I just do what feels right when I hear Michael Jackson music. I learned all of the steps in my Dancing Queen class except the moonwalk. I had to figure that out myself. My friends in class told me to enter this pageant and they even went out and found that red jacket and the hat and the silver glove. Of course that big silver glove is good for covering my knotty arthritic joints, that's a bonus. I never had so much fun for a long time. We still take care of our parents, but life is a lot more fun these days."

"Thank you Jane. Now let's hear from Stephanie."

"Stephanie McCoy. 66. Pendleton. I'm a dog lover, that's what you might not know about me. I have raised nothing but German Shepherds over the years, and most of them have been champion show dogs. The character I am doing in the show, the Pink Panther, is the perfect opposite of my dogs. My husband always liked the dogs, but he was never as attached to them as I was. He's gone now, died almost fourteen years ago. I never wanted to remarry. Being married once was quite enough for me. Besides, I had all those dogs to keep me company. I say most of my dogs were champions because once in a while there was one that was so mellow he just wouldn't learn all the show tricks, all he wanted was love. So what can you do? But some of my dogs won amazing awards. Back when we had a big house, I used the wall of the stairway to my basement for photos of my dogs and their awards. Being dogs, they don't do well with cats, whereas my husband loved cats, and me, well I love cats too. So now you can understand why I chose to be the Pink Panther for my talent. Where else would I get to be a Pink Panther except in the Ms. Senior Tri-Rivers Pageant? And why did I enter the pageant? There was an advertisement posted in the Retirement Village, and my friend Rosemarie dared me to enter. I said I would if she would, and here we are."

Stephanie sat down, and immediately Rosemarie stood up and took a bow. "Yes, I dared her. That's what friends are for, right?

"Oh yes, I am Rosemarie North. 69. Pendleton. Now you all know that Stephanie and I live in the same place, the Retirement Village over in Pendleton. But let me tell you something a little more interesting than that. You know me as an actress, doing Ophelia from *Hamlet* and all. But really, my acting background is as a clown. It's the truth! I never acted in anything before except as a clown. When I was younger I went to clown classes and got my certificate. I was never married, and I liked the idea that I could have fun with kids that way. When you're a clown, you need to figure out who your character is and dress that way, act that way, and think up your jokes and stunts to match that character. My character was Gertrude. She liked to dance but was never very good at it. Her feet kept getting tangled up, and that was what was so funny about her. But she didn't think she was a bad dancer, so she always applauded herself when she finished her dance. The kids would applaud too. They liked her even if she wasn't a good dancer. It's a lot of hard work to dance and be in parades, so one day I decided it was time for Gertrude to hang up her dancing shoes. Oh yea, now the rest of the story. I used to work as a nurse's aide in a hospital. I saw lots of crazy people there, that's how I got the idea for Ophelia. Ophelia doesn't dance but she is as crazy as a clown and it is just as hard to be crazy as it is to be a clown."

Harriet said, "I must admit, I never thought about it that way. The next time I am in a hospital I will look around for clowns. Meanwhile, Helen, you are next."

"Helen Nicholas. 71. Three Points. My husband's name was Dr. Glenn Richard Nicholas. His Ph.D. was in Statistics and Applied Probability. He and I loved to travel, and being at the University we had summers off and could go a lot. We were married for 37 years and visited all of the continents in the world. Our favorite was Antarctica; we were there seven years ago. Then Glenn gradually got sick; he was sick for a long time, with Alzheimer's. It

was devastating. It took him away from me. He got
deeper and deeper into his dark world, day by day.
I stayed with him every day and cared for him until
the end. That was almost four years ago. After that,
I kept pretty much to myself. Entering this pageant
was actually suggested by Glenn's sister. She encourages me to find things to embrace and enjoy. It has
been hard, but I feel good being here among you. All
of you express so much joy. It is a very big step for
me to be here, a day at a time, to get on with my own
life. I've always loved to sing, so I do it in memory of
my husband, Glenn."

"Thank you, Helen." Looking at Carol, Harriet
asked, "Are you ready now?" Carol nodded and
stood up.

"Carol Parcellia. 64. Mercer City. Well, I wish
I had as many interesting surprises to tell as all of
you have. I am a nurse, I work in a pediatrician's
office. It's mostly routine, believe it or not. Children
are a lot more durable than you think. They come
in for checkups and immunizations, they come in
to get permission to participate in certain sports or
activities, they come in with colds and bumps and
sometimes a broken bone. But most of my work is
just maintaining records, setting up for examinations
and talking to the parents if there is a prescription.
One time recently a grandmother brought in her
grandson and we got to talking, and it turns out the

grandma is an old Queen. She told me all about the
pageant and said she would help me if I would enter
it. I am so glad I did. So is my husband, Steven.
He thinks it's pretty exciting to be sleeping with a
potential Queen these days. My kids don't like him
to say that out loud in front of the grandkids, but he
says it anyway. That's about the most unusual thing
I can tell you. Oh yeah, about that Tahitian dance? I
have never been to Tahiti. I just signed up for a dance
class for exercise, and that's what they were teaching.
The teacher loaned me that fabulous costume. She
will be in the audience, probably sitting with my
husband. She wants him to sign up for dancing
classes too. Good luck with that."

"All right, ladies. We are at the last table and the
last speaker. Kate Dearborn, that's you." Kate stood
up and lightly tousled her hair before she spoke.

"Kate Dearborn. 73. Northridge. Like several
of you already said, it is hard to follow such an
esteemed group of women, let alone to be the last
one to speak. But to answer the question about why
I am in the pageant, let me explain. I wanted to wear
a beautiful gown! Seriously, I never knew I wanted
to wear such a gown, but once the idea was out there
I couldn't help myself. I shopped and shopped and
shopped for my gown. I couldn't find a thing. And
then, in desperation, I took to the internet. I invaded
a place called Etsy, which deals only in vintage and

handmade items. My niece told me about it. How many of you shop on the internet? Well, it's all about key words, and before I realized it, my key words had led me into the dark but festive world of Mardi Gras. That's it. Endless black beads shimmering alongside purple and gold and green sequins. I like to believe my gown was worn by a Mardi Gras Queen. When I wear that gown I can feel the good times roll, as they say in French, *laissez les bon temps rouler*. If I had not been in this pageant I might never have had that experience.

"The thing you might not know about me is that I am a writer, a hometown, smalltime writer but a writer nonetheless. This experience, being with all of you, has given me so much to think about and possibly to write about. I've already given some thought to how I would describe each of you in a single word, something that writers like to do." Knowing the ladies would laugh about that, Kate waited before she continued.

"Being with you has given me ideas about how people live with the challenges we all face in life, and how those of us who represent the age of elegance have learned to live life to the fullest. I am so happy to be among all of you, and although I think you should be in awe of me because of my Mardi Gras gown, I am in awe of you. I wish you all the best in your quest to be Ms. Senior Tri-Rivers. Every one of you could be, should be, and will always be a true Queen."

Kate took her seat, glad to have heard the other ladies but relieved that her own story was behind her for now. It had been a long luncheon. Now she was ready to meet Angeline, as planned. She waited while Harriet closed with final thoughts.

"Thank you, everyone," Harriet said. "I am honored and privileged to be among you. Each year I have been involved with the pageant, beginning the year I was crowned and continuing through all the following years until now, I have met amazing women who have lived amazing lives and who bring their charm, grace, gusto, courage, and faith to be a part of this event. While they may enter this competition to win a crown, most of them stay and give fully of themselves for reasons far greater than to win a crown. As they find out along the way, this is a celebration of the age of elegance with other elegant women.

"I want to congratulate each and every one of you for being here, and congratulate you as a group. You are without a doubt the finest we have had as long as I have been privileged to be a part of this event.

"See you next week."

A Matter of Time

Kate and Angeline picked up their things from the dressing room and met outside the Center as planned. "There's a little coffee house not too far from here, how about going there?" said Kate. A mid-afternoon latte sounded good.

It only took a few minutes to drive there, each in her own car. Remembering the cars parked outside the auditorium, Kate recognized the older model BMW. It was Angeline's car. Kate was not surprised; a classy car suited her.

After they parked their cars, they met inside. No longer the funky little gathering place it once was, the coffee house had been remodeled and featured sleek wood panels and stainless steel counters. Out with the old and in with the new, Kate thought. She had seen similar changes to other buildings.

They found a corner booth with molded seats and sat down with their coffee, ready to continue their conversation. "You were just telling me about how you got a job as a clerk in a bank," Kate said. "The Cabots helped you get more education, and then you met someone who helped you get a job in a bank."

"Yes, Mr. Schneider. I will never forget him. He was one of the kindest men I have ever known. He was Jewish. His family had escaped persecution in Europe before World War II. They found refuge here in the United States, and he pledged that he would help others as he had been helped. I was one of many fortunate people he helped. He passed away several years ago, but he will never leave my heart. Because of him I was able to learn all about banking, to move up from one position to another."

"Did you ever meet his family?" Kate asked.

"Oh yes, they were as kind to me as he was. His wife passed away just a year after he did. Not long after that his daughter moved to St. Louis, but she keeps in touch with me to this day. My baby brother and his family also came to the United States with their help. They live in Los Angeles today. I stayed here in the Tri-Rivers region. I never married, never had children. I was so focused on becoming a good citizen, having a good job, and fulfilling my goals that it never seemed like the right time to marry. And then the years went by and I was comfortable, so here I am today, living a very nice life. I fulfilled those goals as best I could. And now I have a new goal."

Kate had to ask, "And your new goal is …?"

Angeline smiled and answered, "To be Ms. Senior Tri-Rivers. It has been my goal for several years now. I made that goal when I saw an ad in the newspaper," she explained. "The ad said women age 60 and over were invited to compete for the title of Ms. Senior Tri-Rivers. But I had to wait. I was only 55 years old when I read that ad. I cut it out of the newspaper and taped it above my desk so I would see it every day. The next year I saw the ad again, and cut it out. By the time I was 60 years old, I had five ads taped above my desk. The very next year, when I was 61, I decided I would take time to watch the pageant, to learn. I came to the rehearsals every week, and of course I attended the pageant.

"I learned a lot. I studied how the contestants dressed, I listened to their philosophy of life and learned how to prepare my own philosophy and say it in just thirty seconds. I paid attention to how the judges interviewed the contestants, to the questions they asked. As for talent, I had to decide what that would be. I chose singing, something I have always loved, and began taking lessons. So here I am now, 62, finally competing. And having a great time, I might add."

Angeline paused before she continued. "Did you know that the winner will go on to compete for Ms. Senior America? Can you imagine how inspiring it is to imagine becoming Ms. Senior America someday? For now, my goal is to be Ms. Senior Tri-Rivers. Then I will set a new goal."

Kate reached out and took her hand. "You

would be such a wonderful Queen, representing all of us who have reached the age of elegance. I wish you all the best," she said.

Angeline squeezed her hand, "I will follow my dreams. I will reach for my goals. It is only a matter of time."

Saturday,
April 5

Realities

On the morning of April 5, Kate checked her list of things to take to the rehearsal. Yes, she thought, I have everything. It was going to be another busy day; the pageant was only a week away. Kate dropped off Lolita at the doggie day care, drove to the highway she now knew so well, merged with the morning traffic, and began another long round trip to the Three Rivers Performing Arts Center.

Muddy clouds blurred the morning sun. There was no rain, but it was cool enough to turn on the heater. She decided not to listen to the radio because she wanted to do some serious thinking.

First of all, she wanted to think about who was likely to become Queen and be honest with herself about what was happening. She knew this was not a beauty pageant, but it was almost impossible to imagine a Queen without beauty, and among the candidates there were several whose beauty was undeniable. Sherry, with her pale, delicate beauty. Angeline, with her dark, regal beauty. Marcia, so perfect in every way. Teresa with her wholesome good looks. Helen, with her sad but lovely face. Even Bonnie in her wild and crazy way. There were plenty of beautiful candidates.

And what about talent? There cannot be a Queen without talent, she thought. Anita's piano talent was delightful, Olga's clogging was amazing, Bonnie was hilariously funny. Angeline and Teresa sang like angels. And Marcia in her red costume was in a class of her own, hands down. Yes, there was plenty of talent among the candidates, too.

Kate could see where this was going. When it came to beauty and talent, she was not among the top contenders, she was not even in the top half. Truthfully, this did not surprise her. What did surprise her was that she felt only the smallest pang of disappointment. She realized that she did not have her whole heart riding on the outcome of this pageant.

In fact, she had been thinking about how she could ever reign as Queen if she were actually chosen. Would she be willing to get up and be on the road like this for the weeks and months in the year ahead? In the Tri-Rivers region there are far flung cities and towns with retirement homes and community centers where visits from the Queen and her entourage were expected. At these venues, wearing their beautiful gowns and crowns and sashes, the court presented little talent shows. Sometimes they rode in parades. Sure, it would be great to keep up the image of graceful aging by making these appearances, but it was also daunting

to think of the miles and months of service ahead
for the Queen. And how often would there be last
minute requests, such as appearances at shopping
center openings, trade shows and special events, she
wondered. Harriet Anderson made it perfectly clear
that the Queen must be ready to go at a moment's
notice, any time at all. Kate continued to think
carefully about the commitment as the miles sped by.
True, she had agreed to all of the duties of a Queen
when she signed up for this pageant, but the reality
was staring her in the face as she sped along on this
cool Saturday morning.

Okay, Kate, reality check is complete, she told
herself. Now you have your cards on the table, your
players on the field, your ducks in a row. You know
where you stand. Does it change anything? Or are
you having a pity party because it is cold and early
in the morning and you're not the prettiest girl at the
ball. And all that fuss about how hard it would be to
be Queen. Ohhhhhh, how sad. Kate smiled at her
clever little talk with herself. "As long as I don't start
talking out loud," she said out loud, and smiled again.
Truthfully, she felt just fine.

"Suck it up, Kate," she whispered to herself as
she entered the parking lot. "Do your duty. Park
the car, and get inside. Time to get to work, and
remember, you are the only one with a genuine
Mardi Gras gown, so suck it up. This will be the only

pity party you will have during the pageant. And don't forget, it's only a week away."

The door to the auditorium was open and Shirley Mortenson was waiting there. "Big hug!" she smiled, arms wide open to greet Kate.

"What's going on?" Kate asked, surprised by the hug.

Shirley didn't have time to answer, she was already busy hugging the next person to arrive and saying, "I feel so excited for all of you, it just seems natural to give you a big hug." She proceeded to surprise each contestant as they came through the door. It felt good to start the day with a big hug, because at 8:00 a.m. sharp, when everyone was seated in the auditorium, Harriet Anderson began with somber news.

"Ladies, the very first thing I must do is deliver some sad news. You may notice that Rosemarie North is not at rehearsal this morning." There was a little murmur among the candidates as they looked around the auditorium, confirming that Rosemarie was not there. Harriet continued, "I am very sorry to report that she has dropped out of the pageant." They waited to hear the reason.

"Rosemarie was being a good neighbor this week, feeding the cat for a friend who was away on a trip. Every morning when Rosemarie opened the door the cat would be there, waiting to be fed. It would rub all around Rosemarie's legs and ankles while Rosemarie made her way to the kitchen, you know how cats can do. As Rosemarie told us at the luncheon last week, she is not as nimble on her feet as she was in the days when she was Gertrude the Clown, and on Tuesday morning the cat got tangled in her legs and Rosemarie fell down, bang, right on the marble floor in the entry.

"She fell so hard she could not get up – you all know that advertisement, don't you? Well our Rosemarie couldn't get up, so she hollered for help until someone heard her and came to see what was going on, and there she was on the floor in a lot of pain. They called for an ambulance and she was taken to the hospital where they did an x-ray and found she had broken her hip. She was immediately scheduled for hip surgery and was operated on the next day. She's going to be in rehab for a while before she is allowed to go home. Rosemarie is so sad to drop out, but she is a spunky gal and says to tell everyone that she is going to be fine and will be back next year to try again. She says the rehab will probably help her to get up and down during her performance as Ophelia."

Everyone clapped, which was a strange thing to do when one of the contestants had broken her hip, but they did. Harriet Anderson had a get well card in her hand, which she waved over her head as she announced that everyone was welcome to sign it. The chatter of the morning was subdued as the card was passed around. No one ever thought that anyone would have to drop out from an injury, let alone hip surgery. It was indeed a reality check.

With great determination, Harriet Anderson said, "And now ladies, you know what they say. The show must go on, so let's go on with the show!"

Black and White Discovery

Fortunately, Kate had pulled out the registration packet early in the week and reviewed the contents. When the packet of information first arrived, she put a paper clip on the instruction page for black and white costumes. Today was black and white costume approval day.

Black & White Costume Requirements
You will need an outfit for the opening and closing ceremonies. Hopefully, most of you will already have the black and white items required.

The opening ceremony of the pageant is the first introduction of all of the candidates to the audience. It is the first time all candidates stand together before the audience, side by side on the stage. It is always an exciting kickoff to the evening. Everyone wears black and white outfits, no fancy gowns, no costumes, just simple black and white outfits. You will wear these same outfits for the closing ceremony. Please select your outfit according to these guidelines:

White top - Stretch top, T-shirt, blouse, sweater or jacket okay. Long sleeve, elbow length, short sleeve okay. No sleeveless. White only. No off-white, ivory, mixed colors or print. '

Black bottom - Skirt or Slacks in black only. No dark gray, no tweed, no stripes or patterns.

Skirt - No floor length skirt, no mini skirt, no full or circle skirt.

Slacks - No jeans, no capris, no shorts, no pedal pushers, no harem pants.

Shoes - Black shoes only. Flat shoes or high heels, either is okay. No wedges, mules, backless, flip-flops, slippers, hiking boots or tennis shoes.

Accessories - Small earrings okay, white, black, silver, gold, pearl, rhinestone. No large earrings, hoops or long dangles. Simple headbands and hair clips okay. No masks, no hats. No necklaces. No scarves or shawls. Plain black belt okay. Pantyhose. Plain, natural color. No black, striped, patterned.

Kate had easily located all of the items in her closet and packed them in her suitcase. Like the rest of the ladies, she left them in the dressing room until they were told to make the costume change.

"After sharing that bad news about Rosemarie, it is time for us to move on," said Harriet Anderson. "Let me welcome all of you to the final rehearsal before the big day, which is of course, the pageant itself, next weekend." Everyone applauded.

The guests in the audience were still getting settled, scattered about in the auditorium. Anita's husband was there as always, as was Myrna's boyfriend. Various others accompanied the contestants from time to time, and this week was no exception. "Once again, we welcome our guests." Here the audience applauded and Harold and Mr. Nick whooped. "However, I hope you all know that next week the rehearsal is closed to everyone except participants. So plan your day, ladies and gentlemen, we enjoy having you here, but this is the last day the auditorium is open to all of you until the official pageant next week.

"Today we will practice the opening ceremony. I trust all of you ladies have your black and white costumes with you. Ladies? Raise your hands." All hands went up. "Very well, let's get to it. Please go to the dressing room and change into your outfits. I trust there will be no deviations from the list of acceptable items. Those were pretty explicit instructions, weren't they? If the guidelines seem like overkill, let me put it this way: you would not believe the things we have seen. I hope we won't see anything other than attractive black and white outfits today. If we do see something unusual, you can be sure you will be asked to change. Please be dressed and back here in 20 minutes, which will be 8:30 a.m."

The dressing room was familiar territory now, and every woman had her space. It just worked itself out that way. Anita sat at the end dressing table on the far left so she would have plenty of room for her long legs. Bonnie enjoyed being in the middle of everything. Kate and Angeline sat more to the right end, and the others set up at various places in between. Teresa used the smaller, more private area at the back of the room and dressed with her back to the group. Sherry also used a more private area in another area at the back of the room. The dressing room was large enough to accommodate everyone and had plenty of garment racks, tables, chairs, and other places to spread out and be comfortable. There were just twelve large makeup mirrors with theatre lighting, but everyone easily moved in and out to use the mirrors when necessary.

Friendships had grown with each week until now there was a great deal of laughter and talk among the ladies. Seeing Teresa and Sherry off in their own private areas was not unusual. Nor was it unusual for Marcia to dress in the ladies room down the hall. "You won't be able to do that the night of the pageant," Harriet advised Marcia one day, "but for now it's just fine." Everyone had her space and everyone seemed happy.

Teresa adjusted the prosthetic in her white bra as she prepared to dress in her black and white outfit. The instructions to wear all white and black pleased her because she already owned the perfect garments. Her cowgirl shirt was white cotton cut on the bias, long sleeves with cuffs, two button down breast pockets, and the typical scalloped stitched yoke. The snap closures on the front and the cuffs were white mother of pearl. The long tails of the shirt tucked nicely into her dress twill cowgirl pants. These were not jeans, she emphasized, they were twill pants. With them she wore a black belt, and her nicest black cowboy boots. She left her white cowboy hat on a nearby chair because wearing a hat was not allowed. She finished adjusting the white bra and turned around to pick up her white shirt.

As Teresa would tell Kate later, it was then she noticed Sherry in her typical spot in the back of the room. Sherry seemed distressed. She was already wearing a white turtleneck angora sweater that looked incredibly soft, and a simple black skirt. She already had her shoes on. But even though she was fully dressed, she turned over the clothes in her suitcase, shook them, and dug under them to look for something. She ran her hands down her sweater and skirt, searching. She shook her hair, leaning to her right side as if to shake out something. Teresa watched as Sherry fell to her knees and moved her hands to feel beneath the chair, the table, and all around her little dressing area.

After snapping closed the mother of pearl buttons on her shirt and tucking it in, Teresa walked over to Sherry. "Can I help you with anything?" she asked.

Sherry did not respond. She kept searching, her head down, her hands sweeping back and forth on the floor. Suddenly she saw Teresa's black boots and looked up in alarm. "Oh, I didn't see you there!" she said.

Teresa bent over to be closer. "I'm sorry. I was just wondering, can I help you?"

Sherry's hands stopped, she had located something on the floor. She grasped it in her left hand and used her right hand to help herself to her feet. "Oh, thank you so much," she said to Teresa, "I think I found it." Whatever it was remained clutched in her hand. "Yes, I've found it." She smiled at Teresa and used her other hand to smooth her hair back into place. "Thank you, Teresa. I'm so sorry I bothered you," she said in her whispered voice.

"Oh it is not a bother at all," said Teresa. "Let me know if there is anything at all I can do." And she went back to her dressing area.

Teresa could not help but look back at Sherry to be sure she was okay. Once again Sherry had seemed so flustered, so unsure of herself. That was when Teresa saw Sherry take the small item from her hand, put it on the table and gently wipe it clean before she lifted it to her ear and slipped it in. To anyone else it would look as if she was putting on her earrings, no one would pay any attention. But to Teresa, the small gesture, the twist of the fingers and the gentle pressing into her ear, followed by adjusting her hair around her ears, made her very certain of what she had seen. It was a hearing aid which had fallen to the floor and she had recovered it.

"Everything about Sherry's behavior is becoming clear to me," Teresa said in a low voice when she located Kate across the dressing room. "When you get a chance, let's find a place to talk."

Kate sensed the urgency in Teresa's voice. "How about now, we can slip outside for a few minutes. I'm ready for rehearsal, and it looks like you are too." They walked down the hall and out the exit door. Teresa quickly described what had happened.

"I am pretty sure Sherry does not know I saw her put the hearing aid in her ear. She obviously did not want anyone to see. She has been so careful about keeping this a secret from everyone."

Kate answered in a whisper, "I am so sad, it must

be very difficult for her. Now we know why she has had such problems in the rehearsals." Taking Teresa's hand in hers, she continued, "I don't think there is anything we can do now, but thank you for sharing this, for trusting me with such a delicate secret. I think our best mission will be to be alert, aware and if there is a time when Sherry needs help, we will know it. Until then, let's pray that everything goes well for her."

With a squeeze of her hand, Teresa nodded her agreement. Then she added, with a smile, "Let's hope all goes well for us too, because it's just about time for all of us to be back in the auditorium."

Kate continued to think about Sherry. She did not know if Sherry wore one or two hearing aids. She thought they must be the kind that were hardly noticeable, the kind that were worn inside the ears because she had never seen them. Of course, Sherry's soft hair always floated around her ears, covering them. Kate wondered if there are times when hearing aids just don't work well, or, as happened just now, are there times when they fall out? Perhaps when she slipped the sweater over her head it pulled the little device from her ear. That was why Sherry felt her sweater, her skirt and finally fell to the floor searching. Sherry was hearing impaired, Kate was fairly certain. Now she was about to perform for an audience. All Kate could think of was how much she hoped there would not be a problem with her hearing aids today or next week in the big event.

At 8:30 a.m. the ladies gathered on the stage, all in their black and white attire. Once again they stood behind the curtain. "Your names will be called, one by one, in alphabetical order. Please step forward and walk all the way to the front of the stage. There is no microphone this time, just walk all the way to the front. Anita Archer, when you get to the front of the stage turn to your left and walk all the way to the end. Olga Asamova, you do almost the same thing – walk all the way to the front of the stage but turn to the right and walk to the end. Myrna you follow and turn to the left, Judith Ann to the right and so on. Is everyone clear? "

"Is that what they call a peel-off or something?" Jane asked.

"I don't know," said Harriet, "but it sounds official, so let's peel off to the left–right–left–right, every other person. How's that?"

"Yes Ma'am," said Jane, with a mock salute. Everyone was ready to go.

"Wait for your name to be called before you take your turn to walk on stage, is that clear? Everyone wants the same moment in the spotlight. When your name is called, smile and step out there and wave at the audience as you walk forward. The next name will not be called until you peel off to the left or right and walk to the end of the stage."

It took a couple of times to get the sequence and the turns correct. The hardest part was exiting the stage after all fifteen women were lined up. "Anita, you will be on the left side so you turn and exit stage left and everyone else who turned left will follow you off the stage. Olga you turn and exit stage right and the others will follow you." Sherry was next to last on the left side. Kate glanced over to see how things were going. She saw that Sherry was getting along fine. With great relief, she decided to try to put aside the thought of Sherry's hearing aids.

Harriet Anderson had just a few comments. "That was excellent, Ladies, and you all look quite beautiful in your black and white outfits. I thank you for leaving your Bermuda shorts and your bowling shirts at home. Not that there is anything wrong with them," she joked. "No changes for your black and white outfits, all of them are approved."

Looking at her watch, Harriet announced, "Fifteen minutes, everyone. Then back to the auditorium." Kate wondered if she heard just a touch of weariness in Harriet's voice.

As everyone trudged back down the hall to the dressing room, Myrna said, "When we first came here, I wondered where the dressing room was. Now we've been back and forth so many times, I think I could find it blindfolded or in my sleep. Hey, maybe I can catch a few winks walking back and forth."

Step by Step to the Finale

The rehearsal progressed to the next item on the agenda. "Let's pretend it's pageant day," said Harriet Anderson. "You have been introduced in your black and white outfits. You have changed into your gowns. You have presented your Philosophy of Life. You have modeled your gowns. You have just finished the talent portion. What now? It's time for the grand finale. It's time for the high point and the end of the show. It's time to crown the new Ms. Senior Tri-Rivers, and it will be one of you!"

It was such a build up the audience burst into applause. Harriet took a bow. "Thank you," she smiled.

"Let's go over the basic structure of that part of the pageant. I'll go through each part, one step at a time."

Most of the ladies had pen and paper ready to take notes. "That's great," said Harriet, noticing the way everyone was prepared. She picked up her own notes and one by one went through each item, reading her notes then speaking extemporaneously about the steps.

"The curtain closes on the last talent act," she began. "Most of you will still be backstage because you want to see how everything goes and that's just fine. She gestured at Marcia, who was the last performer, and continued. "When that curtain closes on the last act, when Marcia is finished, everyone goes back to the dressing room and changes into black and white outfits."

Harriet paused to let everyone make their notes.

"Toss those talent costumes aside, you won't be needing them and you can fold and pack them later. Concentrate on getting dressed in your black and white outfits. While you are changing there will be a little performance by last year's Queen. Our MC will introduce her, and she'll perform. That's all the time you have to get changed into your black and white outfits.

"Line up behind the curtain, alphabetically. Come out on the stage the same way as you did for the opening ceremony, one at a time when your name is called, wave and smile, and peel off to the right or the left. Everyone will cheer because this is the end of the show, and they know that the choice of the Queen is finally going to happen. Then, leave the stage."

Harriet watched as everyone hurried to keep up with their notes. "Yes, leave the stage and hurry back to the dressing room and change into your gowns. Toss those black and white outfits aside and concentrate on getting into your gown. You'll have to hurry.

Now you will be glad you have had so much practice changing clothes.

"While you are changing into your gowns the Master of Ceremonies will be singing a couple of songs. You'll be able to hear him in the dressing room so you will know how things are moving along.

"When you have changed into your gown, your jewelry, and your shoes, come back to the stage and stand in line behind the curtain."

Kate raised her hand. "What order do we stand in?"

"Good question. Remember how you were arranged according to height for the photo in your gowns? Anita, you are the tallest. You will be in the middle. Myrna and Teresa, you are the shortest, you are at the ends. Everyone else, please remember – line up according to height."

"Thanks," said Kate. She made a note and so did all the others.

"The curtain will open and all of you will be there in your gowns. The audience will applaud. Smile, wave, and then wait. Stand still while the next part happens. In fact, you will stand still for most of the rest of the program."

"Stand still, but smile and clap, doesn't that sound like fun?" Bonnie quipped. Everyone laughed, including Harriet. "Sorry," said Bonnie, "I couldn't resist. What's next?"

"The Master of Ceremonies and I will be in the

center of the stage. He will have one list of names in his hand. He will have a different list in mine.

"I will call the names of the winners of the three special categories: Ms. Congeniality Tri-Rivers, Ms. Elegant Tri-Rivers, and Ms. Inspirational Tri-Rivers. If your name is called, please come forward and accept your award, then go back to the line. The rest of you will applaud, but stay in line.

"The Master of Ceremonies will explain to the audience that he will call the names of the five finalists for Queen, as chosen by the judges, in no particular order. If your name is called, please come forward and wait. The rest of you applaud. Unless your name is called, stay in line."

Kate took more notes as they went along. She thought this should be easy for her, but she was writing as fast as she could. She hoped she could make sense of her notes later.

"The five finalists will be asked one question each, as submitted by the judges. You will have thirty seconds to answer the question."

Myrna's hand shot up. "Thirty seconds? That's the same amount of time as our Philosophy of Life, right? That's not very much time."

Harriet smiled. "To some people it seems like a whole lot of time. Thirty seconds, that is all." Myrna did not laugh her typical big laugh. She looked very serious.

"The five finalists will stay up front while the

judges score the answers to the questions. Everyone else stay where you are: in the line behind the finalists."

Kate visualized what that would be like. Fifteen candidates will be on the stage. Five will be announced as finalists. They will go to the front of the stage. Ten names will not be called. Those ladies will stand in line at the back of the stage. She sketched a little visual to help her remember.

"There will be a delay, a waiting period while the judges add up the scores. The MC will talk about how great the pageant is, and so on. Then he will introduce the outgoing Queen. There will be some music. The outgoing Queen will walk across the stage and back, in front of the five finalists, waving at the audience as she walks.

"By this time the judges will have decided who will be the new Queen, and who are the runners up. They will give that list to Charlie, the Master of Ceremonies."

Myrna's hand shot up again. "You mean no one will know until the judges give the note to Charlie? Not even you, Harriet?"

"That's right, Myrna. It really is a secret ballot. I will be as excited to know who the new Queen is as you will be.

"Charlie will announce the 4th Runner up, and she will be given a trophy and a bouquet of flowers.

If your name is called, take your trophy and the flowers, and step back a few steps.

"He will announce the 3rd Runner up, and she will be given a trophy and flowers. Step back.

"He will announce the 2nd Runner up, and she will be given a trophy and flowers. Step back."

Everyone knew what was coming next. They waited for Harriet to make the final announcement, as it would announced at the pageant.

"There will be two women left in front of all of the others. After a lot of buildup by the Master of Ceremonies he will announce the 1st Runner up. Of course that means that the last woman left is the winner, the new Queen!"

Bonnie applauded. The others joined in the fun, smiling and clapping.

"The outgoing Queen will take off her crown and put it on the new Queen. The new Queen, wearing her crown, will be given a trophy and a dozen red roses and will walk back and forth across the stage to music just as the former Queen did. The runner up will take her trophy and flowers and step back with the other runners up.

"MC Charlie O'Day will bring the program to a close and invite the audience to come up on the stage to congratulate all of the participants. It could be pretty crazy, and as they say in the cartoons, that's all folks." She set down her notes and looked at the ladies.

"Are there any more questions?" asked Harriet.
A whole lot of hands flew up. "Okay, I can see we
need to go through this again. No problem. Feel free
to raise your hand as we go through the sequence
and ask your questions as we go along. We want all
of you to be ready for the grand finale of the evening
at the pageant next Saturday night."

After the flurry of questions, followed by the
final talent rehearsal, the morning session ended.
"Thank you, everyone," said Harriet. "Drive
carefully, and we will see you next week."

Many thoughts filled her mind as Kate drove
back to Northridge. Each of the contestants had
experienced disappointments, fear and pain during
their lives. Sherry's loss of hearing and subsequently
her fear and embarrassment were understandable.
Perhaps she did not realize that every woman among
the contestants had experienced her own version of
loss, disappointment, even humiliation along her own
life path.

Kate prayed that Sherry would get through this
and would come out achieving what she wanted,
which as Kate recalled was to sing in front of an
audience again, one last time.

Friday, April 11
and
Saturday, April 12

Interviews with the Judges

The Neighborhood Inn was just off the main highway and a great location somewhat central for all of the pageant contestants. Those who wished to stay overnight could get a room, while those who preferred to return home for the night could do that. Kate pulled up to the Inn, ready for the interviews with the judges, then planned to return home that evening. It was a long drive in the dark, but Lolita would be waiting for her, and that left her no choice.

In the lobby, a poster pointed the way to the meeting room where the contestants would meet with the judges. Those who were not directly involved in the pageant, such as spouses, friends, and relatives were not permitted to join this event. Everyone understood it was going to be a long evening. "No one goes home or back to their room until all of the interviews are finished. We're all in this together," explained Harriet. To entertain the candidates while they waited there were snacks and beverages and a large screen TV. "Plan to be here for about three hours altogether," she said, even though each interview was only about five minutes.

Eleanor Butler was there to help. Kate hurried

over to thank her for the beautiful silk shawl, but Eleanor brushed it off saying, "A good shawl is hard to find. Glad you found one."

When Kate tried to say something more, the old Queen just said, "Pick a number for your interview." Slipping her hand into the bag with the numbers, Eleanor said, "Do you feel lucky? Well do ya?" Kate did a double take, wondering if that was really what she said. "I said pick a number," she repeated with a frown. Kate drew the number seven, which was fine with her as she did not want to be either first or last. "I'd say that puts you right about in the middle, then," said Eleanor.

The judges were in a room across the hall. No one would meet them until their own interview began. All that was known was there were five of them, no one knew who they were or what their questions would be. "Relax. Just go in and enjoy it. They don't bite," was the advice given by all of the old Queens who were there to help and support.

The candidates had been advised to wear an outfit they would normally choose for job interview or a television interview. For most it had been a while since a job interview, and with the exception of Marcia, who was frequently interviewed about art and artists, most were not likely to have been on television lately. That left the choice of appropriate attire to the individual, and each chose something different. For Kate, whose closet was full of comfortable clothes, the best thing she could think of was black slacks, beige sweater, and pearl necklace. She added a brown and black scarf with a red border just to give it a little pop, a word she recalled with a smile. She paid particular attention to her makeup and gave her hair an extra tousle but still wore the comfortable black shoes with the square heels.

Suits or dresses with jackets were popular choices for the interview. No one wore anything with a wild print or pattern. Jewelry was kept to a minimum, no bling. A few of the contestants really stood out in their interview outfits. Myrna looked very serious in a long, black sheath with short sleeves and a mandarin collar and her black patent leather boots. Teresa had traded her jeans for a khaki skirt and the same fitted cowboy jacket she'd worn to the luncheon. She'd pulled back her dark brown hair and clipped it into a large tortoise shell barrette. For the first time since the competition began Teresa was without her cowboy boots, wearing a pair of low heels instead. Kate had to look twice to believe her eyes. Bonnie was chic in a white dress with long sleeves, big black buttons down the side, and a black belt.

To no one's surprise, it was Marcia who stole the show with her interview outfit. She waited quietly at the side of the room, gazing out the window rather than chatting and snacking with the others. She wore a tailored navy blue blazer buttoned at the waist with a single brass button; a crisp, pale blue linen blouse with an open collar; a gold chain necklace and small gold earrings; and flared, lightweight wool slacks in a pale cream color. Her shoes were navy blue pumps with thick cork high heels. She was a picture of elegance and it all seemed so natural and easy. Her black hair was shiny and fluid, as pretty as any shampoo commercial ever seen on television.

It occurred to Kate that with all of her travel and work with museums, it would be fun to talk to Marcia and hear about television interviews while the rest of them waited expectantly, wondering what it would be like. Kate joined Marcia in a seat beside the window. "What number did you draw?" she asked.

Marcia unfolded the little paper and looked at it briefly, as if she did not quite recall. "Fourteen. And you?"

Kate still had her slip of paper in her hand, and said she had number seven.

"Oh," Marcia said in a matter of fact way.

Hoping to strike up a conversation, Kate said, "Well, it should be interesting. Do you think it will be like a television interview?"

"I have no idea," Marcia said, smiling. "But good luck." She turned to look out the window again.

One by one the contestants were called to the

room across the hall. And one by one they came back with great smiles as they exclaimed, "It wasn't so bad. They were quite nice. They didn't ask any weird questions. No, I can't tell you what they asked because they requested that we keep the interviews private, at least for now. Don't worry, they didn't bite."

"Kate Dearborn? Number seven? Please come with me." A cheerful man wearing a plaid shirt had been sent to get her. "How are you doing?" he asked, leading the way to the room with the judges. She replied that she was doing just fine, although in fact she felt very nervous. Panicky. That was the word she'd chosen for herself a few weeks ago. I guess it still works now, she thought.

He opened the door to the room across the hall, and there they were, three men and two women, smiling great big pageant smiles at her. "Come in! We don't bite."

They fired off their questions rapidly: "What is something in your life you are very proud of? What is something you would do differently? Why do you want to be Queen? As a woman of your generation, what message would you give to the younger generation? And the final question: What do you want to be in five years?"

Later, when everyone was allowed to discuss the questions and their answers, Myrna shared her answer to the final question. "When they asked me what I wanted to be in five years, I told them "Eighty!""

When Kate returned to the meeting room, the big screen television was on with the DVD of last year's pageant playing. There were all the beautiful contestants in their gowns, delivering their Philosophy of Life and modeling their gowns as they crossed the stage, smiling and waving. There was Olga! Kate took a second look. Olga looked a lot different. What Angeline had said about learning from participating in earlier pageants was evident, even though Olga looked darned good on that big screen TV. The program rolled along. Soon it was time for the talent. A singer was first to perform, followed by a tap dancer, a guitarist, then Olga, who was number four. She clogged her way around the stage wearing an ethnic embroidered skirt and peasant style blouse. The music was not familiar. Kate agreed with Angeline. The changes Olga had made for the pageant this year seemed to make a big difference.

It was after 9:00 p.m. when Harriet entered the room and announced, "Ladies, the interviews are complete. I've just talked with the judges. You all did great! Now you can go back to your rooms or home to your own beds. We will see you at the Performing Arts Center tomorrow morning. Good news, you don't need to be there until 9:00 a.m. I repeat, 9:00 a.m. I don't think I need to remind you but I will anyway: bring everything, everything you need. You will be busy all day tomorrow and won't be allowed to leave until the pageant ends tomorrow evening. Any questions?" Not a one. It was almost 9:30 p.m. and no one wanted to stay any later. No questions.

"Have a great evening," said a tired-sounding Harriet Anderson. It had been a long six weeks for everyone, maybe especially for her. Even her usually perky hair had drooped. The contestants picked up their purses. Some of them kicked off their shoes and changed into tennis shoes or sandals. They said their goodbyes as they put on their jackets and headed out the exit doors.

The DVD of last year's pageant was still playing although the sound was muted. The Queen had just been crowned and was making her walk across the stage, waving and smiling, carrying a big bouquet of red roses.

Behind her were all the contestants who did not win. They were smiling too.

Pageant Day
Saturday, April 12

Kate pulled into the parking lot and looked at the door to the Performing Arts Center. This is it, she said to herself, you made it. Pulling her suitcase out of the back seat she rephrased her thoughts. Well, you made it this far, the day of the pageant. Now you have to get through this day, and what an exciting day it will be, she assured herself.

"I can't believe the day is finally here," said Bonnie as she tugged her suitcase through the door.

"I can," said Myrna, "but I can't believe Harold and I didn't get a room here after the interviews. We drove all the way back to Northridge last night, then this morning we drove all the way out here again. At least we have a room tonight. I can't believe the day is finally here when we can stop driving back and forth to Northridge."

The contestants found a notice posted on the door of the Performing Arts Center. It was the complete schedule for the day.

MEET IN AUDITORIUM @ 9:00 A.M.
Please be prompt!

Ms. Senior Tri-Rivers
PAGEANT DAY SCHEDULE

- 9:00 a.m. General meeting in the Auditorium.

- 9:30 a.m. Dress in white tops/black bottoms, full makeup

- 10:00 a.m. Photos in black and white outfits

   Practice grand introduction in black/white outfits

- 10:45 a.m. Change into gowns

- 11:00 a.m. Gown practice

   Practice entry from back of stage

   Practice Philosophy of Life

   Practice modeling

- 12 noon Break

   Lunch in cafeteria

   Possible media interviews

- 1:30 p.m. Talent rehearsal

   Wear talent costume and make up

- 3:30 p.m. Makeup and hair as needed

- 5:50 p.m. On stage in black and white

- 6:00 p.m. Pageant

   Grand introduction

Formal gowns and Philosophy
of Life

Talent performances

- 8:30 p.m.   Selection and crowning of
Queen
- 9:30 p.m.   Post-Pageant Party – back stage

No host party. Everyone invited,
family & friends.

Harriet Anderson was in good spirits. "Good
Morning! How is everyone today? Are you excited?"
Lots of clapping. "Good, it's going to be a wonderful
day!" She wasn't wearing her gown and sash yet, but
she was dressed in a long knit skirt, loose top and a
bright scarf. Her silver hair was noticeably perked
up from the night before, teased and sprayed into a
particularly beautiful style.

"Let's go over the schedule for the day, the one
you saw posted on the door when you came in. It's
posted in the dressing room now. We want to be sure
everyone to know what to do, when to do it, and
what to wear."

Harriet reviewed the schedule for the day. "The
morning will go quickly," she predicted. "We will
break for lunch in the cafeteria at noon." And they
did.

Kate stood in line at the cafeteria with Teresa
and Anita, waiting for the ladies in front of them to

finish their selections. Looking around the room she noticed a man talking to Harriet Anderson. Next to him a woman with a video camera recorded the conversation. The camera was clearly labeled KZAP Tri-Rivers News. It was Channel 14! The candidates had been told that news reporters might stop by to do a story on the pageant, but Kate was surprised to see them at lunchtime. "Look at that," said Bonnie, "the news reporters for Clark Gabriel's evening news. My wish has come true. We are going to be in his face!"

Smiling into the camera, Harriet explained how the pageant came to be, how many years it had been going, and other information. Then she motioned to the candidates: "These are the ladies who will be putting on the show tonight, and one of them will be crowned Queen!" she exclaimed, gesturing widely.

The camera quickly turned to capture the ladies sitting at the table with Harriet: Sherry, Stephanie, Anita, Judith Ann, and Angeline. Attracted by her beauty, no doubt, the reporter and camera zoomed in on Sherry. "Can you tell us who you are? What will you be doing in the pageant tonight? What do you think of the pageant?"

Sherry smiled shyly, lowered her eyes, turned her head and answered, "I'm so sorry, would you excuse me?" and she slipped out of the chair.

They turned to Anita, who was happy to answer. "The best thing about the pageant," she exuded, "is becoming sisters with such fabulous women. We are a sisterhood! And for a woman with five sons, that is a miracle."

Next to her Stephanie nodded, "Yes, a sisterhood of sorts. My best friend isn't here today . . ." she started to say. The cameras cut away.

The reporters glanced around, hoping for a more exciting interview. As if on cue, Marcia Van Horne slipped into the seat vacated by Sherry. "Hello, I'm Marcia Van Horne," she said with great energy and a perfect pageant smile, holding out her hand to greet them. Aware of the possibility of reporters being present, Marcia was dressed in a camera friendly combination of a red V-neck top trimmed with charcoal gray and matching charcoal gray slacks. The sheen of her black hair was accentuated by the bright camera lights. Kate and the others moved closer to hear the interview.

"Yes, this is much more than a beauty pageant," she was saying as she smiled into the camera. "It is more about the women we have become in our lives, not the young and beautiful women we once were."

The reporter replied, "I see nothing but beautiful women here," and Marcia flashed her smile at him.

Turning to Angeline, the reporter asked her name and her thoughts about the pageant. "Angeline Zolta. To me it is an opportunity for women of the age of elegance to show what elegance truly means," she said. "Elegance is acquired from life experiences and in many forms. These are all truly elegant women."

The reporter turned to the table behind them. Kate could not hear the rest of the interviews but when she looked back, Marcia had picked up her things and moved to the other table where she pulled a business card from her purse and handed it to the reporters. "I am the Chair of the Board of the Modern Art Museum," she flourished, "which will be a real asset if I am selected as Ms. Senior Tri-Rivers."

After the lunch break, everyone prepared for the final talent rehearsal. The reporters packed up to leave. "We got some great footage," they told Harriet. "We will be back tonight to see who is crowned Queen."

Marcia picked up her things. "Excuse me," Marcia said, brushing by Kate on the way to the dressing room. "I might as well wait in here now that they are gone."

The afternoon practice sessions went flawlessly. Everyone was thrilled and relieved at the prospect of a similarly flawless evening. At 3:30 p.m. they returned to the dressing room, realizing the days and weeks of rehearsals and practice were done. Only the real thing, the pageant, remained.

Suddenly, things began to happen.

"Can I have everyone's attention please?" It was Olga. She held two small tiaras in her hands. "I would like to take this moment to honor the real

Queens of the dressing room, our wonderful Happy Hookers." Everyone clapped. "Please step forward so I can place these crowns on your very worthy heads." With much surprise and laughter, they stood in front of Olga. "Thank you for keeping us hooked and zipped, for watching over our coats and dresses and jewelry while we are away, and for everything else you do."

"Can I have your attention also?" It was Judith Ann, tapping her cane on the floor to get out attention. "My grandchildren sent this box of Star cookies for all of us because they say we are all stars. Please take the cookie with your own name written in frosting. Every cookie is a star except one, which is a cat, a pink cat, for the Pink Panther." Everyone clapped.

"Excuse me everyone, can I have your attention too, please?" It was Sherry. She was carrying a large flat box containing a variety of fresh cut roses. "Danny delivered these for me," she said as she carefully removed them from the box. In her soft voice, almost a whisper, she said, "I hope you will like the roses I have chosen from my greenhouse, they remind me of you." And to each woman she gave a rose as she called her name:

"Stephanie and Carol. The light pink rose is for grace and gentleness.

"Anita and Judith Ann. The dark pink rose is

for appreciation.

"Jane, Bonnie and Kate. The yellow rose with a red tip is for friendship.

"Sandi. The lavender rose is for enchantment.

"Helen. The deep burgundy rose is for beauty and devotion.

"Marcia. The red rose is for excitement and beauty.

"Myrna and Olga. The orange rose is for enthusiasm.

"Teresa. The yellow rose is for new beginnings.

"Angeline. The white rose is for purity and humility."

Harriet Anderson entered the room just as Sherry finished giving the roses to everyone. "I am so sorry to interrupt this occasion, and I do mean that sincerely, but we still have some work to do."

Along with two old Queens, she stepped into the center of the room and continued. "The stage lights will be very bright tonight, and they will simply wash the color right out of your face unless you wear plenty of makeup. We are here to check your makeup. We are here to help you look your very best!"

With that, they began to circulate among the dressing tables, checking each candidate for adequate makeup. They were the cheerleaders. "Don't be shy!" they said. "More blush! More eye shadow! More, more, more makeup! When you think you have enough, put on some more!"

Kate wondered what Kevin would think if he could see her now. Perhaps he would admire her eyebrows, her red lips, her artfully tousled hair. Kate hoped he would be proud of her transformation, small as it might seem to him. Personally, she felt fabulous.

There was a knock at the door of the dressing room. A Happy Hooker, wearing her new tiara, answered the door and turned around to announce that there was a man at the door with a delivery. She asked if everyone was dressed, and could the delivery man come in. She opened the door wide, and there he was in a brown uniform mostly hidden behind a huge bundle of thick white cone shaped flowers with bright golden stamens and long heavy dark green stems. The stems were gathered together and exquisitely wrapped in chic brown paper tied with a raffia cord. The bundle was meant to be carried cradled in the crook of an arm.

"Flowers for Ms. Marcia Van Horne," he announced. "Where would you like them?" Marcia showed the man to her dressing table. He laid down the flowers carefully and quickly said, "No tip, Ma'am, it was taken care of."

Marcia stopped him, "Would you read the card?"

He slipped it from the small white envelope.

"Yes Ma'am, it says "To my little Queen." He set
down the card and backed out of the room.

"Calla lilies," said Marcia, standing back to
admire them. "From my husband, Chad. He knows
they are my favorite flower. They became famous
when Diego Rivera painted huge bundles of them.
Aren't they lovely? But I can't leave them here beside
the dressing table. I won't be using the ladies room
down the hall today, so I need this spot to put on my
makeup." She looked around the room for another
place for the flowers. "There's a place. I can put them
over by the door on that table. They will be out of the
way." She picked up the bundle and moved it.

Kate marveled, "Out of the way? Those flowers
are the most beautiful I have ever seen." She was
glad that the flowers were still visible for everyone to
enjoy.

The excitement built as reports filtered back to
the dressing room that the audience was arriving and
the seats in the auditorium were filling up. Secretly,
cell phones began to emerge from purses and pockets
to receive good wishes, text messages, and photos,
mostly selfies. All phones were supposed to be turned
off; no one was to talk on their phones during this
time. Nonetheless there were a quite a few whispered
conversations by those who could not resist a call
from a grandchild, friend or husband.

Various details came back from people who

peeked through the curtains to see the audience. Myrna's boyfriend Harold was in the front row wearing a green jacket for good luck. Carol's husband and her dance teacher were there. Kate's sister Colleen was in the audience with her daughter Megan. Bonnie's friends sat together wearing huge dark glasses and knit hats in honor of their Mildred. Teresa's son and daughter waved a big sign that read 'Cowgirl for Queen!' Jane's fans wore big foam hands, the kind worn by baseball and basketball fans at games, which were painted white with silver sparkle. Sherry's husband Danny sat in the third row, wearing a white tuxedo jacket with a pink rose boutonnière. Angeline's friend, the daughter of her esteemed employer Mr. Schneider, had come all the way from St. Louis to support her.

Anita got a call on her cell phone from her husband, Mr. Nick. "He says he is sooo nervous," she said, "but when I asked him why, he just moaned. He moaned!" She rolled her eyes and said, "Men."

And Helen placed a framed photo of her husband, Glenn, on her dressing table.

One by one everyone gathered at the door. Dressed in black and white outfits, they waited for the cue from Harriet to move to the stage.

"Just look at those flowers," said Anita, admiring the bundle of calla lilies on the table beside the door. "Marcia, can we put them on top of the piano? They are so beautiful everyone should see them."

Marcia picked them up and handed them to Anita, "That's fine with me. Enjoy."

On the way to the stage Anita cradled the bundle of white calla lilies in her arm the way they were meant to be carried and placed them carefully on the piano as she passed by.

At 5:50 p.m. everyone was on the stage, behind the curtain in a single line, in alphabetical order, wearing perfect makeup, perfect hair, and big smiles. At 6:00 p.m. the outer curtains parted, the music began, and the audience cheered. Standing alone in the center of the stage, Harriet Anderson reigned supreme, stunning in the same lacy silver gown she wore on the first day she introduced herself to the pageant contestants, adorned with huge bling, and her gleaming white sash.

"Ladies and Gentleman, I am Harriet Anderson and it is my pleasure to welcome you to the Ms. Senior Tri-Rivers Pageant!"

Let the Show Begin

As the music played, Harriet Anderson was joined
by the MC. He introduced himself, smiling at waving
to the audience. "Good evening and welcome! I am
Charlie O'Day, your host for the evening. And the
luck of the Irish is with me tonight, such a lucky man
am I to be your host!"

He quickly moved to the introductions of the
candidates. "Ladies and Gentlemen, I know why
you are here, and it's not to see me. Soooooooo,
these are your candidates for Ms. Senior Tri-Rivers.
The center curtain parted just enough to allow each
woman to step onto the stage. "Please welcome Anita
Archer. Olga Asamova. Myrna Brenner . . . . ." He
introduced them, and one by one they came from
behind the curtain in their black and white costumes,
waved, walked across the stage, peeled off to the
right or to the left, and after a final hurrah, exited the
stage.

That was it. It was over. The very first part
of the pageant was over! It was like a blur, it had
happened so fast.

Along with everyone else, Kate hurried from
the stage and down the hallway. Inside the dressing

room everyone unzipped and pulled off their black
and white outfits, put on their pageant gowns and
jewelry and shoes, and restored their makeup and
hair. Getting dressed in her Mardi Gras gown was
simple for Kate. With one slip over the head and one
zip up the back, she was in it, and with one tousle of
her hair, it was restored.

She marveled as she looked around the flurry of
activity in the dressing room and listened to the great
cacophony:

"Was the auditorium full?"

"I couldn't see the audience, the lights are too
bright!"

"But did you hear them? Can you believe how
they cheered for every single one of us?"

"I heard a wolf whistle. Was that your husband,
Carol?"

"That went so fast!"

"I forgot to wave until I was almost off the
stage."

"I could hear my grandkids doing a little cheer!"

"Somebody out there has a noise maker, like a
New Year's Party."

"That's Harold! He's the party guy!"

"Can you unbutton this? I can't reach it!"

"Why are you wearing a blouse with buttons in
back?"

"Darn, I got a run in my pantyhose. Do you
think anyone will notice?"

"I can't remember a word of my Philosophy of Life."

"Me too. I am just drawing a blank!"

"Oh my God, where are my earrings? I thought I left them right here!"

"Hooker? Happy Hooker please!"

"Did my hair get messed up when I pulled this over my head?"

"Help, I can't find my other shoe!"

"I wish I could lose both of mine."

"Somebody zip me up please!"

"Anybody got any chocolate?"

"Can I borrow somebody's hairspray?"

"Can I use this mirror?"

"I am so nervous. I can't believe I am so nervous."

"You look fabulous. Beautiful!"

"You've got lipstick on your teeth. Here, wipe it off."

"This is so tight I can hardly breathe."

"I can't bend over to buckle my shoes. Help!"

"Here, tuck that little ribbon thing inside your dress."

"Did you see Charlie O'Day? He's all dressed up in a tuxedo!"

"I hope he can pronounce my name right, no one ever does."

"You look gorgeous."

"Performance order or alphabetical order? I forget which one!"

"Alphabetical, sweetie. This is Philosophy of Life. Performance order is when we perform."

"Oh my God, I didn't know platforms could be this tall!"

"Where is Kate? Kate? Can you help me?"

"Coming!"

Kate hurried over to help Teresa. To Kate's surprise, Teresa did not need any help. She was dressed in her gown and white boots and simply stood there with her arms wide open, glowing and beautiful. "This is it, Kate, we did it! I just want to give you a big hug to celebrate. As far as I am concerned, all of us are Queens!"

"Yes, all of us," smiled Kate. "Everyone."

Lined up and ready to go on stage for the gown modeling and philosophy of life segments of the competition, Kate admired each of the candidates.

Anita Archer was tall and radiant in her purple gown with silver dots, the dress with an empire waist and long flowing sleeves, the one which she had sewn herself. "Thank heaven this will be the last night I have to wear these silver shoes," she said. "If I am Queen I am going to decree a ban on silver shoes."

Standing right behind Anita was Olga Asamova, who dazzled in her brilliant royal blue gown with rouched sleeves dropped off the shoulder. Delicate blue ribbons on her shoes were the perfect touch.

Myrna Brenner was gorgeous in her emerald green dress with the floating thing down the back. Her shiny black patent leather platform boots added an air of mystery to the dress. "You can wear boots like these anywhere," she claimed. Her red hair was particularly well spiked and showed off her big green bling earrings.

Judith Ann Cole's baby blue prom style dress floated in two layers. She wore it with a baby blue shrug sweater and blue satin shoes. Kate smiled when she noticed a blue ribbon wound around her cane, the long fetters fluttering down the side.

Bonnie Gabriel, in bright red lipstick, was stunning in a red strapless gown, her neck adorned with a huge gold and rhinestone necklace. Her gold platform shoes made her suddenly quite tall. "See, I told you I was delicious. To me, tall is delicious. In these shoes, no one can deny it: I am tall."

Helen Nicholas's elegant beauty was enhanced by her burgundy gown with a black lace bodice and elbow length black lace sleeves. A black lace rose on a jeweled clip adorned her hair. She wore only the most simple makeup, a pale gloss on her lips.

Stephanie McCoy wore a hot pink dress. "I want them to remember I am the Pink Panther," she said. "That, and the truth is, this is the only dress I could find. I really didn't feel like running all over town to find something else. I like it, so it doesn't matter if anyone else does." Pink lipstick and bold black eye liner were the perfect match for both gown and costume. Her black shoes closed with rhinestone buckles.

Sandi Meredith's coral-touched makeup complemented her coral sleeveless dress with a black diagonal scarf that fell across her shoulder and floated down the back of her dress as a train. She had mastered the art of walking with it, sweeping it gracefully behind her.

Jane Morrison shimmered in a royal blue strapless dress and elbow length black satin gloves, "the better to hide my arthritis with, my dear," she explained. Her black satin shoes were decorated with blue jewel toe clips.

Carol Parcellia sparkled in a turquoise satin sheath with cap sleeves and a floor length silver tulle overskirt attached to her waist with a wide silver cummerbund.

Teresa Rodriguez wore the white crepe gown draped over just one shoulder, a turquoise garland circling her hair, and white cowboy boots with gold tips. She gently touched the gold wedding ring on a delicate chain around her neck. "It makes me feel like he is here with me," she explained.

Sherry Springfield dazzled in a clinging dress of gleaming silver. Long silver satin gloves graced her arms, ending just above her elbows. Her silver shoes glittered. "She still reminds me of roses," whispered Kate. "Is there such a thing as a silver rose? Or is it just that chain of silver roses she is wearing around her neck?"

Marcia Van Horne stood tall and resplendent in her purple chiffon gown adorned with silver beading, the Bob Mackie dress everyone had waited to see on the day of gown approval. It fit her perfectly, reminding Kate of a star making a runway appearance. Her silver stilettos clicked on the floor with each step. "Those shoes are high, really high," groaned Anita. "How does she do it?"

Angeline Zolta was exquisite in a gold backless dress with a halter top, both daring and tasteful. Her bronze gladiator shoes were a bold punctuation. In her calm and regal manner, she stood quietly and patiently, ready for her appearance on stage.

Kate herself was quite pleased with her Mardi Gras dress. It felt as enchanting as she hoped it would, glittering just as she had imagined. Her lips were the brightest red they had ever been. No one noticed her sensible black shoes, but everyone noticed hers was the only black dress with hundreds and hundreds of sparkling beads.

As they watched in small groups backstage, Kate and the others were amazed by the applause and cheers that greeted them as each took her turn on stage in her gown and delivered her Philosophy of Life. Even more amazing to Kate was the feel of the rich weight and glamour of her own beaded Mardi Gras gown beneath the bright stage lights, the "Oooohs" and "Aahhs" when she first stepped on stage, and how smoothly the delivery of her own philosophy and her modeling went.

"I can't believe it was so easy," she said. "I didn't stammer once!" She was amazed and relieved that her fear had disappeared. Panicky? That is not the word to describe me tonight, she thought.

Kate spotted Teresa and Sherry but decided she should not bother them. She would wait to share the excitement. She moved around to the other side of the stage, finding a spot where she could see and hear both of them. Soon Kate was joined by others who also wanted to watch.

Meanwhile, eight old Queens carefully and quietly entered the back stage area. Four gathered on each side, ready to perform their dance routine while the candidates changed out of their gowns and into their talent costumes.

Everything seemed to be moving so quickly. Teresa finished her philosophy and after receiving Anita's hug, she found Kate. Both of them watched Sherry, anxious to see if everything was okay. "No problem," Teresa whispered with relief as Sherry concluded her philosophy, exquisitely modeled her silver gown and exited the stage into Anita's arms.

Marcia captured the audience with her beauty, confidence, and Bob Mackie designer dress. Angeline concluded the segment with charm and grace. Anita hugged them all as they hurried off stage.

As the candidates rushed down the hall to the dressing room to change into their talent costumes, the MC could be heard bantering his introduction about the old Queens who were about to perform. "Let's welcome these beautiful dancing ladies, all of them former Ms. Senior Tri-Rivers Queens!"

A Whole Lot of Talent and More

Being first in the performance order, Anita needed to be ready for the talent performance before everyone else. Both of the Happy Hookers helped her pull the purple dress up over her head without messing her hair and makeup; handed her the black slacks, silver blouse and white dinner jacket; and arranged her hair to go under the top hat. "I have never undressed and dressed so fast!" she laughed, slipping her feet into the silver shoes. She paused in front of a mirror to get a quick look, and was almost at the door when Kate stopped her to give her a hug as she left the dressing room.

"Hey, one good hug deserves another," said Kate, to Anita's great delight.

"You cute little Mardi Gras munchkin," she said. "Oooops, I already called you that. Thanks for the hug!"

Anita hurried down the hall. The music of the dancing Queens reverberated from the stage. They had not finished yet; she had plenty of time. The stagehands stood by to push the piano into place. Pointing to the bundle of calla lilies arrayed on top of the piano one of them asked, "Shall we take these away?"

Anita patted the flowers gently, arranging them. "No. Please leave them here for everyone to enjoy."

The old Queens bowed to the audience after they finished their dancing routine and exited the stage. The stagehands pushed the piano to the front of the stage, near the audience while the MC introduced the talent portion of the pageant. "Ladies and Gentlemen, you are about to enjoy the multi-talented candidates for Ms. Senior Tri-Rivers. Does anyone here like piano roll blues? Then let's hear it for our first performer, the lovely Ms. Anita Archer from the beautiful town of Colby!"

Just as in rehearsal, Anita burst onto stage and delivered her rollicking performance of "Piano Roll Blues." Mr. Nick whistled and cheered louder than anyone in the audience, except perhaps her five sons.

Stephanie McCoy was wildly enjoyed for her antics as the Pink Panther, and Judith Ann Cole stood at the mic and sang like an angel in pale blue, *a cappella*. Olga Asamova took the stage with dazzling energy and gave clogging the whole new image she had planned. "Do the math!" shouted her family.

Seated at a table at the side of the stage, a sound technician monitored the lavalier microphones requested by six of the performers. While the standing mic was operated from the sound booth at the rear of the auditorium, each lavalier mic operated independently. To avoid any overlap or confusion, each mic was clearly labeled with the contestant's name on a large tag in separate sections of a large board: Angeline, Teresa, Helen, Myrna, Sandi, Sherry. When a performer was on stage, her mic was turned on. When she finished, it was turned off. After the completion of all of the performances the contestants unclipped their lavaliers and returned them to the sound tech.

Angeline awaited her turn to perform. The small lavalier was almost invisible attached to the shoulder seam of her white sheath.

"Ready?" the sound tech asked Angeline.

"Yes, thank you," she replied, and he switched on the mic. Angeline walked onto stage as the introductory notes to "Unforgettable" began. With her usual grace and poise, she smoothly delivered the song.

The applause for Angeline was still ringing when the MC stepped forward to introduce the next act, Carol Parcellia, Tahitian dancer. "Watch out, ladies and gentlemen, this lady has a whole lotta shakin' goin' on!" Secretly, Kate suppressed a groan.

Teresa waited in the wings, her white hat in her hands, her guitar on the strap across her shoulder. Her lavalier was clipped to the collar of her shirt and as soon as Carol finished, the sound tech signaled Teresa that the mic was on. Closing her eyes and taking a deep breath, Teresa was ready. "Okay," she said to herself and opened her eyes. She put on the white hat, touched the wedding ring that hung around her neck, and walked on stage exuding a grace and confidence that captivated the audience even before she strummed the first notes of "They Were You."

"I couldn't help the tears in my eyes at the very end," she said as she exited the stage. "It didn't change the song, it was just those very last words, in Spanish. I hope no one noticed."

Anita hugged her, "I noticed, but it just made the song more beautiful."

By now the audience was laughing at Bonnie's character, Mildred. Then the auditorium became hushed when Helen appeared on stage with her candle and sang the lovely "Sunrise, Sunset." Kate waited a moment after Helen left the stage before she walked out to the stage microphone. Without hesitation, without tripping on her words, and with the dignity they deserved, she delivered the two poems by Robert Frost.

Afterwards, Teresa gave Kate a hug before Anita could get to her. "That was wonderful," she said.

"Thank you," Kate replied. Looking around she added, "Isn't it wonderful that everyone is doing so well? Can you believe how this is going? It's perfect!"

Energy was high as Jane Morrison danced to Michael Jackson's song, doing another new version that she improvised as she went along. No one knew; they loved it.

"Only four more acts," said Kate as Jane exited the stage.

"Ladies and Gentlemen," proclaimed MC Charlie O'Day, "if you have ever been to New York, you are in for a special treat. Or even if you haven't, here she comes, Lady Liberty of New York, New York, Ms. Myrna Brenner!"

Myrna's mic was switched on. The music to "New York, New York" was cued. Right on time, right on the beat she pranced onto the stage in her spiked crown and platform boots to the cheers from the audience. As soon as she started singing, whoops of delight filled the auditorium.

Seated in the front row, hair slicked back into a shiny pony tail and resplendent in his green jacket, Harold shouted, "You got it Babe, you got it!"

Sandi Meredith blithely "swallowed" the dinner knife and smoothly switched the sugar packets and ended her magic act with a flourish of the two spoons. The stage hands removed the magician's props and the table from the stage.

Sherry was next. MC Charlie O'Day joked with the audience. "Our next performer, Ms. Sherry Springfield of South Mercer, asks the question "Shall We Dance?" She better not be asking me, because I can't dance! But I think she has a King in mind, like

The King and I, which of course is fitting for a Queen. Let's welcome Ms. Sherry Springfield!"

Teresa and Kate stood together where they could see Sherry perform. "There she is," whispered Teresa when she spotted her.

"Oh no," said Kate, as she watched Sherry. "She looks terrified!"

The sound tech nodded to Sherry indicating that the mic was on. He waited for her signal to begin the music. Sherry did not signal nor make her entry.

The audience was confused. First they clapped for Sherry but when she did not enter, they stopped, asking each other, where is she? The MC stood near the side of the stage, Harriet Anderson next to him. "Sherry Springfield," he announced again. "Let's give her a big welcome." A few people clapped, but most waited for her to make her entrance.

From their vantage point near the sound technicians, Kate and Teresa could see Sherry begin to search through the folds of her dress, looking, looking. The sound tech watched and waited for her signal. None came.

Kate watched with great alarm. "What's happening?"

"She lost her hearing aid again, I'm sure of it!" said Teresa.

Sherry checked both ears, probing. It seemed she still had one hearing aid. Looking at the sound tech, she nodded the signal for the music to begin. Her lavalier mic was attached to the sleeve of her gown and picked up her words as she stepped onto the stage, saying "oh no, oh no." Looking one way, then the other, she appeared lost on the stage. The first notes of "Shall We Dance?" were playing, but Sherry did not sing a word. Finally she held up her hand. The sound tech stopped the music. The stage and the audience were silent.

"What is she going to do?" Kate asked with distress, sharing the fear that Sherry must be experiencing. Teresa pulled off her white hat and threw it aside. It skittered across the floor, disappearing in the darkness. She lifted her guitar and took it off her shoulder, carefully removing the blue shoulder strap, and handed it to Kate.

"Kate, you have to take this. Please put it on and keep it for me! There is no time!" Her white boots flashed as she ran across the darkened back stage, rushing to the sound tech, who was waiting for a signal from Sherry. "Please! You must turn on my mic!" cried Teresa. "I'm Teresa, please turn on that one!" She pointed to the switch marked with her name. "Sherry needs help! Please start the music for her and turn on my mic!" she repeated. The sound tech quickly understood the urgency of the situation and turned on Teresa's mic and the music.

Teresa dashed to the side of the stage, stopping

just behind the curtain. She closed her eyes and took a deep breath. "Okay," she whispered to herself and walked onto the stage. Knowing the lyrics of "Shall We Dance?" very well, she sang the few introductory verses.

Sherry, on the opposite side of the stage, looked up and saw her. She knew. She understood. Lifting her taffeta skirt lightly off the floor, she walked toward Teresa, who continued to sing. They met in the middle of the stage, and slipping her arm into Sherry's, Teresa finished the opening verse.

Sherry regained her composure. She could see Teresa singing, watch her lips, hear her with the one hearing aid which was on the side where Teresa stood next to her, facing the audience. With a flourish, Sherry turned toward the audience and soared into the song, her lovely voice capturing the imagination of those in the audience who knew this song so well. Teresa stepped slightly back, just behind Sherry. Her mic still on, she sang along with her.

Back stage Kate let out a loud cheer, "Way to go girls!" She did not notice the stage hand hissing shhhhhh, but soon he realized what was happening too. Probably no one heard Kate's cheer, as the music played on. Everyone was delighted as Sherry sang and danced the little loops.

Marcia had been waiting far to the back of the stage, alone. Now she emerged to get ready for her own performance which would be after Sherry's. "What's this?" she exclaimed when she saw Teresa and Sherry on stage together. Looking at the two of them in disbelief, she demanded, "What are they doing?"

Who can blame her, Kate thought. She is next and this is really unexpected. Kate wasn't sure how this would affect Marcia until she saw her making her way to Harriet Anderson, who had stepped back stage during the crisis.

"This is unacceptable!" she said angrily, marching up to her.

"Do you hear me?" Marcia raised her voice. "How could you let them do this?" Her voice was shrill now. She clenched her hands and screamed at Harriet Anderson. "Aren't you going to stop them? This is highly irregular!"

Sherry and Teresa held hands as the music ended and the audience began to clap. Perhaps the people back stage had not noticed Marcia's outburst. Perhaps they pretended not to hear, or maybe they really didn't. Perhaps the sound of Marcia's voice was lost in the applause.

No one said a word. Except Harriet Anderson.

"Yes Marcia, it is highly irregular," Harriet agreed, her voice low, steady, and firm. "But sometimes the show simply must go on, and sometimes it requires a little help."

Quickly, Harriet Anderson turned to the sound technicians. "Nice work," she said, "now please turn off all of the lavalier mics. All of them. Now! We don't want any distractions from a stray mic. And please notify the technicians to turn off the stage lights the moment those two ladies, Sherry and Teresa, are off the stage. Marcia Van Horne is about to dance. Her performance begins when the stage is totally dark. The techs know the routine. Tell them that everything must be perfect for Marcia Van Horne's performance."

Turning to her she said, "I'm very sorry, Marcia. If anyone can do this, you can. Break a leg!"

MC Charlie O'Day kept the audience entertained as the stage was prepared, and he promised that the final act which they were about to see would be red hot. "This lady will turn the heat up, so get ready for Ms. Marcia Van Horne of Devonville!" In the blackness of the stage, one spotlight came on. Marcia was the center of everyone's attention as she smiled gloriously and struck her pose, hands on her hips. The rhythm of the music soon had the audience clapping with her.

While Marcia dazzled and danced, Kate made her way down the hall to the dressing room. She wondered what the judges would think about Sherry's performance and about Teresa stepping in to help her. She wondered how it would affect their decision. It would be a tough call. Sherry could not have continued alone. Would it have been better to let her fail? Or did Teresa do the right thing for Sherry and the pageant?

Anita and Judith Ann embraced the sad and weeping Sherry in the dressing room. Kate, still wearing the guitar on the strap, looked for Teresa. She found her at the back of the dressing room, sitting silently in the shadows.

"You were wonderful to do that," she said slipping her arm around Teresa's shoulder. She took off the guitar and handed it to Teresa.

"Thank you," said Teresa, lost in thought.

"Are you concerned about how the judges will react?" It was almost time for them to vote.

"I don't know," said Teresa, "but I could not stand by and let Sherry fail. I just couldn't let that happen. It's all about love. That always comes first."

Regrets, Apologies and Last Call

"I am so sorry," Sherry wept as some of the ladies clustered around her. "I almost wrecked everything you have worked so hard for!" She looked around the room for Teresa and Marcia. "If it wasn't for Teresa, I don't know what would have happened. Marcia, I am so sorry! I hope I did not ruin anything for you."

Harriet Anderson burst into the room, cutting Sherry's apology short. Her entrance had such force and power that everyone was suddenly silent. Charlie O'Day could be heard introducing the outgoing Queen who was going to perform. Harriet held up her hand and raised her voice. "We have no time for talk, ladies. None! Is that clear? We are on a schedule regardless of what occurred a few minutes ago. Put that out of your mind. Get out of your talent costumes. Get dressed in your black and white clothes and let's get on with the show!"

She looked around the room, glaring at each candidate. "Focus on what lies ahead. The new Queen is going to be crowned. We have no time

for anything other than our show. Any questions?"
Hearing none, she turned and abruptly left the room
to hurry back to the stage. The outgoing Queen was
still performing.

Kate took Sherry by the arm and hurried across
the room to the area where she usually dressed.
Sherry was trembling.

"Help, please, can we have a Happy Hooker
over here?" called Kate. "Don't worry, Sherry, everything is going to be okay. You just need to get back
on stage and finish the show."

The Happy Hooker came quickly to help Sherry
change from her costume into her black and white
outfit. Sherry squeezed Kate's hand. "Thank you. I
won't let anyone down, especially now." Kate rushed
off to change into her own black and white outfit.

Quickly, they joined the others hurrying down
the hall to the stage. Kate watched Teresa hold her
head high and walk with confidence across the stage
when her name was called. Such dignity, she thought.
Kate quietly reflected that she still had not decided
on the single word to describe Teresa. There were
several she had considered. She vowed she would
find the right word soon.

When the black and white review was over,
everyone scurried back to the dressing room to
change into their gowns for the last time.

While the voice of the MC chatted in the

distance, and just before he began singing, Kate zipped up her Mardi Gras gown. In took less than a minute for her to be available to fill in as an extra Happy Hooker. This will be my last time, she thought. Along with the Happy Hookers, she hooked, buttoned and snapped until all the contestants were ready for the final trip to the stage.

"What order are we in this time? I forgot!" Myrna shouted.

"Height," said Anita, patting the petite Myrna on her back. "Calm down, you pretty little thing. Get in line according to height. You're on the far end, remember? Teresa is on the other end and I'm in the middle. God bless you all, this has been so wonderful. I love being in the middle of all of you."

There was no time for a hug as the women hurried to the stage.

And, the Winner Is...

Kate felt the tension as the women lined up behind the curtain. Where usually someone joked, there was mostly silence now except for a few apologies as they arranged themselves according to height.

"Excuse me. I didn't mean to bump you."

"Do you have enough room?"

"Sorry, I need to squeeze in here."

Sherry had hardly said a word since the talent performance ended. Like everyone else, she wondered what the consequence might be. Would she be disqualified? Would Teresa? Would it make any difference at all?

In her silver gown, Sherry took her place next to Teresa near the end of the line. She whispered to her, "Teresa, I can't tell you how much I appreciate what you did for me. Thank you from the bottom of my heart. I pray this won't affect the outcome for you."

Slipping her arm around Sherry's waist, Teresa hugged her and said, "I'm glad I could help." Adjusting the shoulder of her white gown, she whispered, "You know, we all have to face our greatest fears in one way or another." With an extra squeeze – and a smile – she added, "You sure chose a heck of a way to face yours." Sherry smiled back at her. Just then the curtains opened and the audience applauded. The judges would select the new Queen soon. All the candidates smiled and waved. It was part of the show, and the show must go on.

"What an exciting evening," proclaimed Harriet Anderson, standing in the middle of the stage. The sound tech had turned on her mic without being told. A slight trace of the fierce leader she had been in the dressing room just minutes before remained. Poised and charming, she smiled brightly at the audience as she spoke in a manner which clearly conveyed that the show would go on without any more unexpected moments. With great enthusiasm she gestured to the line of smiling contestants. "Let's hear it for these lovely ladies, because all of them are winners!" she said proudly. The audience applauded.

"Among this group of fifteen candidates there are three who have been chosen for special recognition. These three have been selected to receive the titles of Ms. Congeniality Tri-Rivers, Ms. Elegant Tri-Rivers, and Ms. Inspirational Tri-Rivers. The awards are especially significant because these three women were chosen in a secret vote by their fellow competitors.

"The first woman to be chosen is Ms. Congeniality Tri-Rivers. Truly a friend to everyone in the competition, the winner is Anita Archer! Please come forward and accept your trophy, Anita." Above the applause from the audience there was a loud "Atta girl" from Mr. Nick and cheers from her five sons.

"The next woman chosen by her fellow competitors is Ms. Elegant Tri-Rivers. Beautiful, gracious and self-assured, a woman of true elegance, the winner is Angeline Zolta! Please come forward and accept your trophy." Kate wished she could see the audience but the lights were too bright. She was sure the loudest applause came from Angeline's friend, the daughter of the man who had made so much possible for her.

"And finally, the next woman chosen by her fellow competitors is Ms. Inspirational Tri-Rivers. This woman exemplifies all the traits which inspire others and particularly inspire the women of this pageant. The winner is Teresa Rodriguez!" Kate clapped so hard she felt her hands sting.

Teresa accepted the trophy, smiled and waved, and even gave a very slight nod of her head. Kate noticed the gesture and thought it was quite regal.

The three women returned to the line of candidates. "Way to go," Myrna whispered to the three of them as they stepped back. "Shhhhh," reminded Stephanie.

The five finalists were about to be named. Channel 14 news had moved the camera close to the stage. The excitement was like a shiver through the crowd and especially among the contestants. The MC finished his long buildup and now the moment was here. "The final five contestants for Ms. Senior Tri-Rivers, in no particular order, are:

"Myrna Brenner!" She looked at Harold and blew him a kiss, then raised both arms and waved as she walked forward.

"Bonnie Gabriel!" She gasped with delight then rushed forward on her tall gold heels, waving and smiling as her friends in the audience cheered.

"Marcia Van Horne!" She smiled radiantly, turning to one side then the other as she waved and stepped forward to join the other finalists.

"Olga Asamova!" Her family and friends jumped up and down in the audience, shouting "Do the numbers!" as Olga waved and smiled.

"Teresa Rodriguez!" For a moment Teresa did not move, as if she did not expect her name to be called. Her hand went to her neck and grasped the wedding ring on the chain. She closed her eyes, turned and hugged Sherry, and stepped forward.

Kate felt a moment of surprise that Angeline's name had not been called. It was hard for her to comprehend. Then, for just an instant she felt a pang of disappointment that her own name had not been called, even though she did not expect it and had come to terms with it. All of this disappeared as she felt a rush of sheer joy for the five finalists. The judges picked the right ones, she thought, and next year they will pick Angeline. I will be there to see it.

She looked quickly at the faces of the others in line who had not been selected as finalists. Everyone was smiling, of course, what else could they do? What were they thinking behind those bright smiles, behind the makeup? They had worked as hard as the others, they had expressed themselves and dressed themselves in their best possible choices. What was it that the judges saw in the final five but did not see in them? Kate would never know of course, but that was certainly a question a writer might ask someday.

At the moment, the MC was explaining what would happen next. "This hat contains the final interview questions. The judges will consider your answer as they make their final decision. In no particular order, each of you will pick your question from this hat. When your turn comes, you will have thirty seconds to answer. Are you ready?"

With a big smile he announced, "Olga Asamova, you will be first. Marcia Van Horne you are second. Bonnie Gabriel you will be third. Teresa Rodriguez you are forth. And Myrna Brenner, you will be last."

Each finalist pulled a folded slip of paper from the hat and without reading it, handed it to Harriet, who wrote their names on the backs of the slips of paper. "Now, Ladies, please move all the way to the front of the stage, that's right, move all the way up here," said Charlie O'Day, offering his hand to guide them forward. They moved to the front of the stage to be very close to the audience. Harriet read the questions, and he held the microphone for them to answer. One by one they responded.

While the audience could hear the questions and answers of the finalists, the rest of the candidates stood in line at the rear of the stage where it was almost impossible to hear the dialogue. There was nothing they could do but wait. This is what we signed on for, Kate reminded herself. They stood there in a row, on the hard floor under the hot stage lights, sweltering in their gorgeous gowns, aching in their high heeled shoes.

It was their second marathon of enduring the long minutes while the final phase of the pageant played out. Kate thought it was a good thing they had practiced the week before so they would know what to expect. On the other hand, maybe it would be just as well not to know. She loved her Mardi Gras gown but had not expected its ornate gold and purple and black beads to become so very heavy as the minutes ticked by. Even worse, the beads warmed up beneath the intense stage lights and held the heat. Her pantyhose and half-slip insulated her body. Her feet throbbed in her plain black shoes. If she had one word to describe the situation, she said to herself, it would be "miserable."

Carol was visibly perspiring in her turquoise gown, her face damp and red beneath the layer of stage makeup. Next to her, Stephanie stood stoically in her pink dress. "How are you doing?" Carol whispered to her.

"My feet are killing me and I am hot. Hot pink," she replied.

Sandi shifted from side to side, one foot at a time. The black train nestled around her feet, probably keeping the heat inside the dress. She whispered, "So I am not the only one melting under these lights?"

"Are you kidding me?" hissed Jane. "Pretty soon I will be just a puddle. I already took off my gloves. They were just too hot. Even Michael Jackson would take off his glove." Then, with a big stage grin, Jane whispered, "Everyone remember to smile!" They did.

Although they were all hot and hurting, no one in the line at the rear of the stage appeared to be broken-hearted, at least as far as Kate could tell. She realized she probably was not the only one who suspected she would not be selected. All of the others seemed to take the loss well. In fact, most of them did not seem disturbed at all. She looked at Angeline just to be sure. Holding her trophy for Ms. Elegant Tri-Rivers, Angeline turned her head just a little and smiled at Kate, nodding her head very slowly, very slightly, almost imperceptibly. What did that little nod mean, Kate wondered. If it meant what she thought it did, she understood, and nodded back.

With a big round of applause, the MC announced that the judges would now take a few minutes to tabulate their final scores and select the new Ms. Senior Tri-Rivers. The finalists stepped to the side of the stage to wait.

"In the meantime, Ladies and Gentlemen, please welcome our wonderful outgoing Ms. Senior Tri-Rivers as she takes her final walk across the stage!" The music soared "Here She Comes Miss America," and even if it wasn't a Miss America Pageant, everyone loved it. The outgoing Queen, aglow in a ruffled red and black gown, her crown sparkling in the stage lights, walked one way, then back, waving and smiling. The MC glanced nervously at the judges, waiting for a signal that their decision had been made.

In the back, the candidates sweltered beneath the stage lights and smiled and smiled as they watched the Queen walk by, waving. Kate wondered if the smiling women on the DVD of last year's pageant had been as miserable as she was.

"I hope the judges hurry, I can't stand it much longer and Harriet will just have to shoot me if I take off my shoes," whispered Anita.

"Not if I can get her to shoot me first," said Carol, still perspiring beneath the lights.

"Hey, watch what you say," whispered Kate. "Remember, I'm going to write about this."

Carol whispered, "Not if we can get her to shoot you too."

It was difficult to keep from laughing, but fortunately everyone was supposed to smile so this made it a lot easier.

The music stopped and the TV camera moved in even closer. The outgoing Queen stepped to the side of the stage. The audience was silent. The MC stepped forward. Holding up the card he had just received from the judges, he announced, "We have the final tally from the judges, and now the big moment is here! Ladies, please return to the center of the stage."

Resplendent in their pageant gowns, Bonnie, Myrna, Marcia, Olga, and Teresa returned to the center of the stage where they stood very close to the audience and very close together. Bonnie and Myrna held hands. Olga and Teresa put their arms around each other at the waist. In the center of the five finalists, Marcia posed with her hands on her hips. At the side of the stage, MC Charlie O'Day studied the paper with the names of the winners. Harriet Anderson stood with the outgoing Queen next to a table at the side of the stage; on it were five bouquets of flowers, a new white satin sash with the words "Ms. Senior Tri-Rivers," and five trophies of various sizes.

Charlie O'Day finally spoke. "The fourth runner up for Ms. Senior Tri-Rivers is Bonnie Gabriel!" Harriet handed her the trophy and a bouquet of flowers. Holding both of them high, Bonnie smiled right at the Channel 14 News television camera, holding the pose for just an extra moment.

"The third runner up for Ms. Senior Tri-Rivers is Myrna Brenner!" Myrna raised her flowers as high as she had held the torch. The people sitting around Harold had to hush him so he would stop cheering and blowing his noise maker and let the show go on.

"The second runner up is Olga Asamova!" Even with the ribbons on her shoes, Olga couldn't resist a couple of clogging steps after she received the trophy and flowers. Her family was still cheering as she stepped back alongside Myrna and Bonnie.

"And now, the two finalists," he said with great drama. They are Marcia Van Horne and Teresa Rodriguez! One of them will be the Queen, the other will be the first runner up. If for any reason the Queen cannot fulfill her duties, the first runner up will step into her place. Ladies, the best of luck to both of you.

"And the first runner up is," and he waited to say her name, "Marcia Van Horne!" As the audience began to applaud, Marcia looked at Charlie O'Day, her face oddly expressionless. She started to say something to him but stopped. No one knew what she was about to say because she accepted the flowers and the large, first runner-up trophy from Harriet, and stepped back with the other runner-up winners. She did not smile. She did not talk to the others. She stood very quietly, the flowers held loosely in her arm, waiting for Teresa to be named as the winner. She placed the trophy on the floor beside her, not embracing it as the other winners did.

The cheering had already begun when Charlie O'Day announced, "The winner, the Queen, the new Ms. Senior Tri-Rivers is Teresa Rodriguez!" Teresa stepped forward, smiling and waving. The outgoing Queen walked across the stage, lifted the crown from her own head, and placed it on Teresa's dark wavy hair, first removing the small garland of turquoise flowers. Harriet gave Teresa a huge bouquet of red roses, which Teresa held in one arm, and the huge trophy, which she held in the other.

Charlie O'Day tried to stop the happy crowd from surging down the aisle, up the center steps and onto the stage. He couldn't.

"Would everyone please wait for just a moment while our new Queen takes a walk across the stage? It's the traditional Queen's walk. Everyone please wait?" They didn't.

He tried to wish everyone a good evening but no one was listening. The swirl of friends and family and the delight of the reunions between

all of the contestants and their supporters, the
flash of cameras, the joy of "Hi Grandma!" and
"Congratulations" overpowered any closing
ceremony.

Harriet scurried around the stage, gathering
the five winners together. "Teresa, Marcia, Bonnie,
Myrna, and Olga! Please, please wait just a moment!
Dave needs to take a few photos of the five of you.
Please hold your trophy in one hand, the flowers in
the other. Teresa, stand in the center." Click. Click.
Click. It took only a few minutes and soon everyone
swirled into the celebration again. Several trays of
cookies and pitchers of lemonade had appeared on
the side table and everyone helped themselves.

Teresa joined her family, hugging each of
them. Bonnie disappeared into a sea of friends who
still wore big black sunglasses. Myrna and Harold
walked arm in arm around the stage, talking loudly
and laughing. Olga's grandchildren ran around the
stage chanting, "Grandma! Grandma!"

Anita held her husband's hand. Mr. Nick had
joined her on stage and held her trophy. He smiled
broadly as he displayed it: Ms. Congeniality Tri-
Rivers. "They got that right," he said proudly.

"Mr. Nick," groaned Anita, reaching down to
remove her shoes, "if I have to stand in these shoes
one more minute you will have to carry me home!
I am going to take them off no matter what Harriet

says and put them over on the piano. Don't worry. I
don't care if we forget to pick them up later. Better
yet, I hope someone steals them. I won't miss them
when they're gone!"

She pulled them off her feet and made her way
across the crowded stage. The piano was in the
unlighted far corner at the back, pushed out of the
way by the stage hands earlier in the show. Anita
stepped around the curtain and stopped abruptly.
Marcia was in the far corner at the back of the stage,
alone. What was she doing beside the piano, away
from everyone else? Anita waited, not sure what
she should do. Marcia was looking at the beautiful
array of calla lilies still lying on the top of the piano.
She did not see Anita standing by the curtains in the
shadows.

Kate noticed Anita standing by herself at the
side of the stage. "Colleen, would you and Megan
excuse me for just a moment?" she said to her sister,
who was chatting with some of the others on the
stage. "I just want to check on my friend."

She joined Anita beside the curtain, asking
softly, "Is everything okay?"

Anita nodded, "It's just these shoes. I was going
to put them on the piano." She gestured at Marcia.
"Poor Marcia," said Anita in a low voice, "do you
think she needs a hug?"

Kate looked across the black expanse, then

shook her head. "I don't think she wants to be disturbed right now."

The two of them stepped back. They could still see her through the slip of space between the curtains. Slowly Marcia raised her arm, and slowly and resolutely she swept the calla lilies across the piano until one by one they spilled onto the floor. They lay there in disarray. Marcia looked at the scattered flowers for a few seconds, then lifted the bouquet she received as runner up and dropped it on top of the calla lilies. Picking up her trophy she headed for the dressing room and just moments later, still wearing her Bob Mackie gown and silver stiletto shoes, she walked briskly down the hall pulling her small suitcase with one hand, and carrying the runner up trophy in her other hand. The exit door slammed as she left the building for the parking lot.

Anita and Kate looked at each other in amazement. What had she done? And what should we do? They hugged each other and shared the pain they felt for Marcia and their bewilderment.

"We won't tell the others. She was hurt and angry. No one else needs to know," said Anita, adding, "I will go over and pick up the flowers."

Kate nodded in agreement. "Why don't you take the calla lilies home; no one will be surprised because Marcia sort of gave them to you anyway. As for Marcia's bouquet, I will take it out to my car right now. No one will know she left it, no one will know I took it. Unless of course, you would like to have it."

Anita declined. "No, I don't want it. It is so sad. I'll just arrange the calla lilies on the piano like they were. I was going to leave my shoes there anyway, so I will get everything when Mr. Nick and I leave. Really, Kate, as soon as we are done here, you and I must go back to the group and join the party. This has been a wonderful evening. Let's not let anything change that."

Kate and Anita walked across the big empty back stage toward the piano. In the shadows Kate spotted something else. "Wait," she said, and bent down to pick up the white cowboy hat. "It landed here when Teresa took it off and ran on stage to sing with Sherry. I guess she won't need it now that she has a crown. I'll take it to the car now, along with the flowers, and give it back to her later. No need to explain how we found it."

In a few minutes, Anita and Kate rejoined the celebration on the stage. "Is everything okay?" asked Colleen.

"Yes," said Kate, "Anita and I just needed to take care of the calla lilies that were left on the piano."

Good Night Ladies

Kate noticed that no one asked about Marcia during the party. Perhaps it did not seem unusual for Marcia to be gone; during the weeks of rehearsal, she kept to herself most of the time anyway, and rarely joined the others. No one seemed to notice, and everyone in the large crowd was having a good time mixing and talking together.

It was about 9:45 p.m. when Harriet Anderson raised her hands and asked for the attention of the crowd. When all was quiet she began to speak. "I'd like to take a moment to thank everyone," she said, and went on to praise the stage hands, the sound technicians and all the other participants for the success of the pageant. "Without all of you, this pageant would not have been possible." Everyone applauded.

"And now, a word from our Queen."

"Excuse me, please," interrupted Sherry, stepping forward. Her husband, Danny, stood behind her. "I am so sorry, but before the Queen speaks, which is the most important thing of all, may I have a minute to speak?"

Harriet looked at Teresa, who said, "Of course."

Sherry took the hand of her husband and introduced him, "This is my husband Danny. He is my best friend and supporter. He did not want me to be in this pageant because I had not 'come out' about my hearing impairment. He thought keeping it a secret might cause a problem. You see, I am deaf in both ears, a genetic condition that came on recently. He thought I should let you know about it. I didn't want to. He was right. I should have told you. I know now that you would have been just fine about it. I was wrong. I want to apologize for what happened tonight and most of all I want to thank you for your kindness and understanding. I've had a wonderful time and only regret that I did not tell you about my hearing from the start. But now you know, so let's get on with this party. And, forgive me for this pun, but let's hear from the Queen."

"Thank you, Sherry," Teresa said as she stepped forward, her crown sparkling and her white sash a perfect match to her gown. "And thank you, all of you," she said looking from person to person. Everyone applauded. "I would like to introduce my children, my best friends," she said embracing them with both arms, "and these are their families. I want to thank them for their love and encouragement, and I want to thank you for yours. Long speeches aren't good for parties and it is almost 10:00 p.m., so let's put an end to the speeches and celebrate for the last few minutes we are here in this beautiful center. I will miss you all, and I will miss our Saturday meetings, but I will see all of you soon."

~

Colleen and Megan put their suitcases in the trunk of the car and fell asleep in the back seat as Kate drove home that night after the party. Kate's suitcase, her purse, the bouquet of flowers, and the white cowboy hat were on the passenger seat in front. On the long, quiet trip she had plenty of time to think about the questions she had asked herself earlier. What was it that the judges saw in the final five that they did not see in the other contestants? Why did Angeline fall short? Why did Helen? Even Sherry, although her failed performance was certainly the main reason for that. But those were the least of her thoughts.

Driving along the highway that night she wondered, what was it that made them choose Teresa? Why not Marcia? What did they see that made the difference?

Kate believed that Teresa was the best choice, that she would make the best Queen, but how did the judges know that? They did not know about Marcia's outburst back stage before her performance, and no one would ever know about the calla lilies and the bouquet of flowers. But somehow the answer to the question of why they chose Teresa and not Marcia seemed to be reflected in those moments.

She was almost home. Perhaps she would write about those questions sometime, she thought. She certainly would not forget them. Oh yes, and the one word to describe Teresa? That trophy had it right. The word: Inspirational.

After the Pageant

Post-Pageant Party

It seemed like the pageant was a long time ago, even though only a week had passed. Colleen and Megan stayed with Kate for two days, the writing club had a coffee hour on Tuesday in Kate's honor, and no one paid much attention to the flowers Kate brought home and put in a vase in the living room. Kate threw them away on Thursday.

On Saturday, Kate was surprised to receive a letter with the Ms. Senior Tri-Rivers logo inscribed on the envelope. She opened it and read the invitation.

You are Cordially Invited
to a
Post-Pageant Luncheon
in the cafeteria of the
Three Rivers Performing Arts Center
on
Saturday April 26 at 12 noon.
No host luncheon. Casual attire. No rehearsal!
Please RSVP to Harriet Anderson 333/485-7674

"I'd love to come," Kate told Harriet Anderson when she called her. "I would not miss it for anything."

Harriet was delighted. "I know it's short notice, but a lot of the candidates will be there, plus the Happy Hookers, plus Dave, and who knows who else. I've invited the former Queens, although they are not as keen about it as we are. Their schedules are already busy with Queen appearances, but at least a couple will show up. Eleanor Butler plans to be there. So does Shirley Mortenson. We have reserved the area at the end of the room for us."

"One last visit to the doggie day care," Kate explained to Lolita when Saturday came. Her wagging tail showed she did not mind.

The 70 mile trip seemed longer than ever. Kate thought about how glad she was that she did not have to do this every week, realizing again how difficult it would have been for her to keep the schedule of a Queen. She was happy that Teresa had won, and could hardly wait to see her and find out how things were going.

"Things are going great," said Teresa, wearing the sparkling crown and her black twill pants, boots and a western jacket. "My grandson volunteered to stay in the guest room at the ranch when I need to travel. He loves to take care of my horses and dogs. Who knows, maybe he will even move in full time for the rest of my year as Queen. He goes to the community college not far from the ranch, so it would be great. And the truth is, I think he likes the adventure of being away from home, having the place to himself. You know how it is to be young and have all those ideas and dreams."

"Yes, I certainly do," said Kate. She found herself reflecting again, just for a moment.

Kate picked up a large plastic bag she had placed on a chair. "I have something for you," she said as she handed it to Teresa.

Teresa opened the bag and pulled out the white cowboy hat. "Not as white as it was before I threw it across the stage," she laughed. "I'll get back to wearing it next year. Thanks!"

Stephanie held the entry door open for Rosemarie, who came into the cafeteria using a walker. "Don't worry about me, I am doing fine. Stephanie keeps me busy. She says I have to keep my promise to be in the pageant so you can expect me again next year. Maybe I will do my Gertrude the Clown act. It's probably better not to be Ophelia with my hip and all. And besides, Gertrude is funny. Ophelia isn't."

"Where is Anita?" asked Kate. "It doesn't seem right when she is not here to hug us."

Harriet Anderson delivered the bad news. "Anita won't be here today. Her husband, Mr.

Nick, had a small heart attack, if there is such a thing. *Angina pectoris*. It happened a few days after the pageant. Anita is staying at home with him, of course. She sends her love. Here is a card for her and of course for Mr. Nick. I will pass it around for everyone to sign."

"There are some others who can't make it," announced Shirley Mortenson, standing beside Harriet Anderson. "Bonnie is making a cake for a client and can't be here because the wedding is tomorrow. Jane is taking a special Dancing Queen class today. She wants to become an instructor, and hopes to teach women of the age of elegance. Can't you see them all doing the moonwalk? And finally, Marcia sent an email, a letter of regret. She and her husband are traveling in Europe. She wishes everyone well and hopes to see you again, although her schedule with the Modern Art Museum Auxiliary Board is keeping her very busy."

"Let's hear from some of the others now," urged Harriet Anderson. "Let's go around the table, tell us what you are doing."

"My husband and I are signed up to take swing classes – together," said Carol. "I could hardly believe it when he said yes, and now he is more exited to go to class than I am. We have our first class on Thursday evening."

"I'm writing a new song," said Judith Ann. "The

choir sang my pageant song last weekend. It was such an honor. I'm hoping they will sing my new song at Thanksgiving."

"I'm working on some new magic tricks," said Sandi. "I have a gig at my grandson's birthday party. Don't think it is easy to fool a nine-year old kid because it is not. He figured out where that knife went the first time I did the trick for him. So I am practicing a lot."

Olga said one of her grandkids took her trophy to show at school. "He says it proves that math is good for you."

Myrna threw back her head with a big laugh and said that Harold takes the trophy with them wherever they go. "Actually, he shows it to more people than I do. You'd think he was the winner!"

Quietly, Helen said, "I am working on my husband's memoirs. He started them before he got so ill. I am finishing them for him."

"Sherry? Angeline? Kate? What about you?"

"You all know about my roses," said Sherry in her delicate, soft way. "I am experimenting with a hybrid, trying to do it myself. If it works out it will be a rose of many colors, and I will call it The Pageant. And one more thing, I will be getting new hearing aids soon, implants actually, and they won't fall out of my ears. My appointment is next week."

Angeline took a deep breath and said, "I am

getting ready to enter the pageant next year. It's part of my plan." She smiled as she looked at each person at the table. "I hope all of you will come."

And finally Kate said, "I am going to write a book. I warned you! And what's more, I'm going to put a photo of my fabulous Mardi Gras gown on the cover." Everyone applauded.

Teresa tapped a water glass with her spoon and asked, "May I have just a couple of minutes to speak to you as your Queen?"

Everyone answered, "Yes, your Majesty."

First of all she thanked everyone for coming, for their good wishes and their support. "I've only been Queen for two weeks, but it has been great. However, something more happened to me at the pageant. I told you about my scar. I showed it to you. You not only accepted it, you didn't think much more about it. That was the best thing of all. I learned from you that no matter what we face, no matter how deep the scars, there is always love and acceptance.

"From you, because of you, I have decided to go about the business of being Queen without taking extraordinary measures to hide my scar. If a gown or a performance costume happens to reveal the scar, so be it. If I need to wear a tank top on a hot day and the scar is visible, so be it. If someone wants to ask about it, so be it. If no one notices or no one cares, so be it. The scar is not me. It won't be an issue, and it won't be hidden. As women of The Age of Elegance, we all have scars. It may be ironic, but it is part of what makes us all so beautiful. Thank you for helping me accept this, just as my beloved husband did."

Without missing a beat, 87-year-old Eleanor Butler raised her hand and shouted, "And we all say Halleluiah and Amen!"

Was it Worth it?

After hugs and goodbyes all around, and one final group photo taken by Dave, Kate got into her car and began the long drive home. The Ms. Senior Tri-Rivers Pageant is really and truly over, she thought as she drove. No more rehearsals, no performances, no reunions. The Queen is busy doing queenly things, the rest of us are going on with our lives. It was weeks ago when it all began, and yet it seemed as if it passed in an instant and ended so soon. Time. It had that way of passing so quickly.

Was it worth it, she asked herself. Was it worth the time, the travel, the work, the money, and everything that happened? Yes, she thought, yes. It was exciting to take part in all the pomp and parade of the pageant. There were so many interesting moments and people to write about, and stories to tell. And most of all, she met such remarkable women and made new friendships. For all of those reasons, it was worth it.

And the gown! Her glamorous, long, sparkling, and beautiful Mardi Gras gown made it worth it. Without the pageant, she would never have known how delightful it was to wear such a treasure. She

vowed she would find an occasion to wear it again.
And of course, a photo of it would go on the cover of
her book.

Would she enter the pageant next year? No. She
was sure about that. While Angeline had a dream to
become Ms. Senior Tri-Rivers, a dream she should
and would pursue, it was not Kate's dream, and she
would not cling to it. She did not regret the choice
she made when she decided to enter the pageant, but
now she would move on.

Choices. It was like she said in her philosophy
of life: it is best to look at the choices you have and
imagine the possibilities that lie ahead.

Smiling to herself, she suddenly had an idea. "I
do believe the possibility that lies ahead now is just a
phone call away," she said aloud.

As soon as she got home, Kate phoned Kevin's
Salon in Devonville, hoping she would be able to
schedule an appointment. "You are in luck," said the
receptionist. "How about Wednesday at 9:30 a.m.?"

Kate checked her calendar, the one with the
sticker that said KATE. "Yes, that will be great.
Please tell him I need a trim and I'd like to try a little
color. Tell him I am ready for some pop."

Wednesday morning, Kevin streaked a small
amount of Morning Sunshine Glow into Kate's hair,
then snipped, tousled and misted it. He showed her
the latest in eyebrow paintbrushes, and she said, "I'll

take one of those." He added up the total and she signed the little electronic tablet.

As she was about to leave, Kevin opened his arms to hug her. "Kate, I'm so sorry you didn't win," he said.

Hugging him back, Kate assured him, "Oh, but I did, I did!"

About Ms. Senior Pageants

For complete information about Ms. Senior pageants, consult their webpage at *http://senioramerica.org*.

**Philosophy and Purpose of the
Ms. Senior America Pageant**

"The Ms. Senior America Pageant is an exciting combination of talent and inner beauty along with individual fulfillment and elegance.

"More than a "beauty pageant" it is what America is about . . . a re-affirmation of life and self worth, of laughter and tears, of inner beauty and outward charm.

"By giving women 60 years of age and older an opportunity to display their "inner beauty," talents, and elegance, the Pageant seeks to draw attention to the achievements of senior women. The Pageant motivates and encourages women to utilize their full potential and share a positive outlook on life with others. Participants represent a cross section of America."

Senior America, Inc.
387 Herbertsville Road
Brick, NJ 08724 USA
Phone (732) 746-2598
Fax (732) 601-9172